Star

Lee

Blue Saffire

Perceptive Illusions Publishing, Inc.
Bay Shore, New York

Blue Saffire/Perceptive Illusions Publishing, Inc.
PO Box 5253
Bay Shore, NY 111706
www.BlueSaffire.com

Publisher's Note: This is a work of fiction. Names, characters, places, and incidents are a product of the author's imagination. Locales and public names are sometimes used for atmospheric purposes. Any resemblance to actual people, living or dead, or to businesses, companies, events, institutions, or locales is completely coincidental.

Ordering Information:
Quantity sales. Special discounts are available on quantity purchases by corporations, associations, and others. For details, contact the "Special Sales Department" at the address above.

Star/ Blue Saffire. -- 1st ed.
ISBN 978-1-941924-68-6

To my Fru Fru for always encouraging me to be more and do more. There would be no me without you! Love you forever and miss you so much.
—Blue Saffire

CHAPTER ONE

From the Start

Lee

I guess looking back now, it wasn't a lack of mentors and advice that got me caught up. It was the right mentorship and a lack of listening that landed me in my situation. I had plenty of advice, some of which I spent too much time listening to. I almost lost what was important because I thought I was above it all.

I thought like many of you, *that won't happen to me*. I'm here to tell you it will and it can. No matter how smart you are or how smart you think you are it can happen to you. I just hope it doesn't and if it does, I hope you have the opportunity to see your way out of it.

Me, I escaped some things, but not all. I wasn't untouchable the way I thought I was. Maybe the best way to get you to see my point would be to come clean and tell you my story—every detail, my whole truth. I brought someone here with me to help you understand my story from more than one angle, but first I think I should get this started.

My name is Lee Johnson. I play football in the NFL. Ever since I was little, I swore I would make it to the NFL and marry me a beautiful wife, have lots of kids, and my own businesses. I was determined to get everything I wanted.

I entered the game with a plan and focus. I didn't want to be the rookie that got caught up in the game and forgot that there is life off the field. I wanted to be in control of my options.

It's why I was determined to not just go to college. I wanted to take advantage of the education football offered me. After my four-year undergrad and landing my shot in the NFL, I decided to go back to school.

I figured a Masters in Business would help me to start my business or at least get me on the way there. I had no idea that going for my Masters would change my life forever. As I think about it now, school opened the options that kept me from getting lost in the game and the life.

I remember very clearly where it all started. It was my rookie year in the game. I landed a great contract and I was truly at the top of my game. I was playing for the team I wanted and gelling with my offense like we had been playing together for years. I looked good as a rookie quarterback. My dreams were coming true as far as my sports career was concerned. I was on track and heading towards my goal.

I felt it was a good idea not to put school on hold, since my career was going so well. I enrolled in NYU's Business graduate program, determined to get my degree. I was pretty much coasting through the program. School had never been an issue for me. My GPA had never fallen below a 3.8 and I didn't shy away from the more rigorous classes.

I was taking a research and strategic planning course. I'd been excited to take this class. It was what I needed to help me focus on getting my plans in order to finally decide on my business and how to move toward getting it started. I had a few ideas in mind, but nothing solid. I just had this feeling that by the end of this class I would have it all together.

There was this girl in my class, Crystal. She was very beautiful and smart. She'd been in one of my other classes the semester before. I don't know what it was about her, but I would watch her. She was different. She was always focused. I watched her determination in class and admired it. I love a woman with brains and she had it all, brains and beauty.

Crystal, with that flawless brown cocoa colored skin, beautiful brown eyes, and that sexy short haircut—the entire package. I mean the haircut was perfect for her face, the back and left side were cut low, but the right side was long and framed her cute face. I remember I would watch her full lips as she would talk in class. Sometimes it was a little distracting. Her shapely physique was another huge distraction.

She always set up her seat in the same location, no matter the class. She would sit in the middle of the class, next to the middle of the row, taking up at least three seats when she could. Her bag and things in one seat, her laptop on the other and she would sit in the middle.

I'd fallen into the habit of sitting a few rows behind her, where I could get a nice view of her and that face. I guess now it sounds like I'd been stalking her. Nah, I just thought she was pretty. When I didn't need my attention for class, she was a great focal point.

I remember the second session of the research class. The professor had announced that she had formed our groups for the research models. We were to be paired into twos. I sat in my seat praying that Crystal would be my partner. The professor began to call off groups, while I stared at Crystal waiting.

"Gloria Stewart and David Lowery," the professor called. "Crystal Livingston and Lee Johnson, Kristen Harper and Fred Osborn."

I wanted to jump out of my seat and fist pump. I felt the grin that hit the corners of my lips. This would be my chance to get to know her better.

Crystal turned around in her seat to look up at me, two rows behind her. I could see the frown on her face, as she rolled her eyes, turning back around to face the front of the room. I remained happy she'd be my partner.

I would finally have a reason to talk to her. Crystal wasn't the type you just walk up to and think you're going to throw some corny game. I knew I had to come correct.

Some of the other groups moved to sit together right away, but Crystal didn't budge. After the look she gave me, I wasn't going to move either. We sat through the lecture and took notes, until the professor announced we were dismissed to meet up to start planning.

I watched as Crystal packed up her things, heading for the professor's desk. I waited, packing my own things. She had a discussion with the professor, looking up at me a few times with her face twisted with aggravation. This was nothing new to me. I had group partners underestimate me all the time as an undergrad, just based on the fact that I was a jock. After a few minutes she nodded at the professor and made her way to leave the classroom. I picked up my things and followed her out.

"Excuse me, you're Crystal Livingston, am I correct?" I asked, as I caught up to her outside.

"Yes," she replied dryly. "Listen, I talked to the professor. I'm trying to get a different partner. I take this seriously and I think that maybe a switch would be best."

"Wow, Crystal you haven't even given me a chance. I'm no slacker, I get all my assignments done and I maintain a very high GPA, but if you want to jump out of the pan into the fire…it was nice to meet you and good luck," I replied.

I wasn't about to beg her to be my partner. I think that had to be the rudest way anyone had tried to ditch me.

She pressed her lips together, the wheels turning in her head. "Okay wait. The professor does want me to at least try and she did say that you're a good student," she paused and sighed. "Okay I apologize, it's just the last two group projects I did, I got stuck finishing both on my own. I will get an A, Lee, with or without you. I would just prefer if it were with."

"Okay, Crystal, so let's start over. I'm Lee, it's nice to meet you," I said, as I looked into her eyes. I noticed that up close her eyes look almost violet and not so much brown at all. "I will be your research partner and I think it might be a good idea if I gave you my number and you give me yours so we can stay in touch during this process."

I tried not to show my irritation. I could understand where she was coming from. Still, I was a little pissed off at her assumption.

"Okay," she chuckled, as she pulled out a piece of paper to write on. "Here this is my number, but I would like to get started as soon as possible. Are you free tomorrow?"

"No problem, I have practice in the morning, but I'm free in the late afternoon and tomorrow evening," I replied, as I put her number in my phone and sent her a quick text, so she would have mine.

"Please tell me you're not a jock," she huffed.

"Check your phone for my number, Crystal," I laughed ignoring her comment. "Where and when do you want to meet?"

"Ugh! The campus library. I have a class at six, so can we meet at two?"

"Sure, I will be there at two, see you tomorrow," I said as I turned to leave.

I went to get in my Porsche, the second big-ticket item I treated myself to after signing my contract. It was a simple indulgence, a black, 911 Turbo Cabriolet, which I had customized. I made my way home to my first big-ticket item, my condo. A spacious one bedroom, one and a half bath, the perfect bachelor's pad.

I laughed to myself as I drove. Crystal had made some big assumptions. She would see. I planned to more than handle my part of the work, it was my grade too we were talking about. I didn't expect her to be so cold, but I guess I would be too if I got stiffed twice.

When I made it to my condo, I threw the food my chef left in the oven and took a quick shower to relax. I didn't think I'd be going anywhere for the night. I was more focused on getting my head in the game so I could start that weekend. I finished off my dinner and made my way to bed.

CHAPTER TWO

Bring it On

The next day practice seemed to fly by. I was on top of my drills and I had the playbook memorized, thanks to my photographic memory. The coaches were seriously considering letting me start and I wanted to show them I was ready. This was a big step for me. I wanted to do what I came to do, win. It was a great opportunity for me and I was determined to spend the rest of the week showing how truly ready I was.

After practice I looked forward to seeing Crystal. I figured maybe we would start on a better foot. I got to the library a little before two, running right into Crystal, as she made her way inside. As usual she looked great, dressed in a pair of light blue jeans, a pink button down shirt, layered over a white tank top, and a black leather jacket.

"Hey, Lee, you're on time," she chimed. "That's a good sign."

"Whatever, Crystal," I laughed.

I wasn't going to let her get to me.

"We have a lot of work to do. Do you have any topics in mind?" she asked, as we walked into the library.

The assignment was to come up with a business to conduct research on. Once we finished the research, we had to create a strategic business plan to target the same market. I had been thinking about it all day, but I wanted to hear her thoughts. Maybe we could come up with something we both liked.

"I was thinking we could talk about things that interest us and come up with something from there," I responded.

"Okay that will work," she replied, as we sat at a table in the library. "Well, I have a Cosmetology license, that's the field I will be in when I finish this degree."

"Cool, that's how I made money as an undergrad. I have my barber license. I used to cut hair in my dorm." Things were going great, we already had something in common.

"Really? Then this is great. We can do research on customer satisfaction or something," she offered.

"Okay, my friends have a unisex shop. I know they will be willing to help. We can survey the clients there."

"Alright, cool, then we can create a plan to start a shop in that area," Crystal smiled, showing how into our plan she was.

"So, should we get to the research for the lit review?" I asked.
"Sure."

"Do you want to split up or work together?"

"Oh, no, we're working together," she answered, as she wrinkled her nose at me.

"No problem, let's get started," I chuckled.

We started working, using the computers and reference resources. I shocked her, as I found study after study that we could use. I'd even created a quick map of what we needed to find. I could tell she was impressed, despite the fact that she wasn't going to say so. We had about fifty references by five o'clock. That's when her stomach started to talk out loud.

"Are you hungry? I know a great place not far from here. We could get something to eat," I offered.

"No, I have class in an hour. I'm just going to run to my dorm and get something," she replied, as she stretched. "Is it okay if we call it a night? Can you meet me here again tomorrow?"

"Sure, I have practice in the morning, but I can meet you at two. Is that alright?"

"That's great, I'll be out of class by two, so tomorrow. Thanks, Lee," she said, as she packed her things to leave.

"No problem, see you tomorrow," I called, while she grabbed her things and left.

I went home to get started on sorting out the stack of literature we had. I wanted to read through it all and get it annotated. That would cut down on a lot of the process and get us moving along.

I ate while I read, highlighting and making notes at the same time. Once I made it through everything, I rewrote my notes so I could make a copy for Crystal. Not paying attention to the time, I failed to notice it was one in the morning by the time I finished. I went to bed to get in a few hours before practice.

The next day practice was great. I was focused and I won the starting job for the weekend's game. I was amped. I tried my best not to get caught up in that rookie state of mind that some players get into. I was determined to know that I would be starting for the year. It was a lot of pressure being the rookie quarterback, but I handled it well.

Some of the guys wanted me to go out that night to celebrate, but I needed to focus on the project with Crystal. I wanted to keep my priorities straight. I could celebrate when things were truly in order. Starting that weekend was just the beginning. I had a ways to go.

Beating Crystal to the library that afternoon, I went straight to the computers to start finding more references. I had five already when my phone went off. It was a text from Crystal asking where I was. I texted her back my location in the computer area. I was sure she thought I was slacking and hadn't arrived yet. I still didn't think she trusted me.

"Hey, look at you," she chimed, as she found me. "I thought you were late, but you're at work already."

"Yeah," I chuckled. "Here, I annotated the references from yesterday, here are the notes."

"Are you serious? Wow this is great. This is a lot of work, Lee," she beamed, as she looked through the notes.

"I found a couple more so far. I figure if we get through another fifty or so we should be good to move on."

"Cool, so move over. I feel like I need to step it up, you're showing me up," she laughed.

Her shift in attitude was nice to see. The cold shoulder didn't suit her and I wasn't feeling it anyway. We'd get more done without the animosity.

We worked our way through a few more hours to find the resources we needed. I found myself enjoying being so close to her, as we sat side by side. She'd reach across me, smelling sweet, like vanilla and pineapples or something.

We got into a system, she'd print off two copies of everything and I'd retrieve them from the printer. We had a great flow going, knocking the work out quickly. Our combined quick thinking and reading helped out.

Once again, her stomach told on her. I looked at her and laughed to myself. She tried to ignore it at first, so we could finish up. I could see her making faces and rubbing her tummy. Once we had the last few, she looked like she wanted to run for something to eat.

"I really want to help go through these with you this time, but I need to get something to eat," she said, as we printed the last references.

"Sure, no problem," I answered. "You want to grab something and then come back here?"

"My butt is killing me. I cannot sit in these chairs again, but my roommate is already having a study group. Do you want to go to a coffee shop or something?"

"How about we go get something to eat and then we can go to my place," I offered.

"Okay… and I look like I'm going to your place? I barely know you," she snorted.

"Look, this is a lot of work and my place is comfortable. I have a taser in my car, I can show you how to use it," I laughed and gave her a smile to show that I was harmless.

"No, thank you. I have one in my bag and I know how to use it just fine," she answered, pausing to think. "Okay, but I have a black belt just to warn you."

"Okay," I laughed.

"So what are we going to eat? The food budget is getting low for the month, so Wendy's or Mickey D's it is," she chimed, as we picked up our things to leave.

"Don't worry, it'll be my treat."

We went to the parking lot where I parked earlier. On the way, I called to see if I could get us into one of my favorite restaurants. Crystal was always fly, I didn't have to be worried about her not being dressed nice enough to get into the place.

The black slacks, grey blouse and lightweight cropped black leather looked good on her. Her heels were the same grey as the blouse. Yeah, she was dressed just fine.

I opened the trunk for us to throw our things in, before I went to open her door. She climbed in, putting on her seatbelt. I expected more of a reaction to the car, but she seemed indifferent. I was cool with that. Again, I knew she was different.

With our reservations set, I drove uptown to the spot. Crystal relaxed, closing her eyes for a few. I took note that she wasn't very talkative. I turned the music on low, trying to make it seem like I was okay with the silence. I wanted to have a conversation with her, but I couldn't think of anything to say.

When we arrived to the restaurant, the hostess made sure we were seated right away. Crystal didn't look impressed or disappointed. She took her seat giving her attention to her menu.

I decided I would try to start a conversation while we waited to place our orders. She didn't have to tell me her life story, but it would be nice to at least have some type of discussion. I looked over my menu, as I tried to decide on what to eat and what to say at the same time.

She ordered for herself, while I made up my mind and ordered as well. Once the waiter left, before I could think of something to say, Crystal looked across the table at me with curiosity written all over her face. I couldn't help wondering what was on her mind.

"So Lee, how was practice?" she asked to my surprise.

"Great. I'm looking forward to the season."

"So what do you play, might I ask?"

"I play football for the NFL," I answered and laughed to myself. My being drafted was a pretty big deal. I was surprised the name didn't register with her.

"Oh, my little brother is into football. He needs to focus more though. He has the talent."

"That's cool, maybe he would like to come to a game. I could get you guys some tickets. I have the home game schedule in the car. You can let me know which game you want to come to," I offered.

"That depends," she smiled. "Do those tickets come with strings attached?"

"No strings at all."

"Okay, I'll see if he wants to go," she said, with a grin. "What's making you take the classes? Just curious."

"I don't want to count on the game forever. I want to have a business, something I can call my own. The classes are to build a foundation. You?" I returned.

"Well, you know about my license. I want to open my own chain of salons. My dad says I never stick to anything, so I pretty much have been doing this degree on my own. I want to show him I can finish and then open up my first place."

"That's cool. How much longer do you have until you finish the program?" I asked.

"This is my last semester," she said with a huge smile. "So Lee, what's your vision? I mean what's the perfect life for Lee?"

"Let's see...it would be to have a successful career in the NFL, my own successful business, a determined and accomplished wife and lots of kids."

"Nice answer," she said, raising her eyebrow. "Sounds like you think about that a lot."

"Yeah, I'm putting things together. How about you?"

"I want the successful businesses, a determined smart husband, and when all of that's in place I want the children. I want the foundation set by the time I have children. You know?" She said, a pretty smile brightening her face.

"Yeah, I feel you. Well, it looks like you're on your way."

"Yup, tunnel vision," she laughed.

We ate dinner and talked some more. Just like I thought, she was a very intelligent woman. I found myself very comfortable talking to her. I didn't mind her questions. I wanted to answer them and ask her more. We talked mostly about business, goals, things we accomplished so far.

"Tell me about the draft process. That must have been crazy to go through," she said, after a small lull in the conversation.

"I had the support of my mom and a few good friends. To me, that made the difference in getting through it all," I replied. "You know, the support of those that love me."

"Yeah, I bet that did help a lot. It's always good to have a supporting family," she said thoughtfully.

"Definitely," I nodded. "I have my support system and I read a lot to stay focused."

She tilted her head at me with a smile on those gorgeous lips. I could see her assessing me. I watched her back, awaiting the thoughts I could see surfacing.

"What do you read?"

"I like motivational books. Greg Livingston is one of my favorites. He's an ex-player gone entrepreneur and politician. His net worth is ridiculous. That's where I see myself in the future. He has some great books that I've read," I said

Her smile grew while she listened to my words. She seemed to be listening, soaking them in. I liked that I could share all this with her.

Once we finished dinner, we went straight to my place. I made sure she made herself comfortable, as I made myself a place on the plush rug in the living room. She kicked her shoes off and we went to work. We had papers spread out everywhere, on the floor, the coffee table, and the couch. Things seemed to go faster than when I did it by myself. She pulled out some great information and sources.

Just like in the library, we had a flow going on, bouncing ideas and directions off of each other. She was one of the best partners I'd had in a long time. It was like talking to myself. We were highlighting the same things to show each other, cracking up once we saw we were on the same page. I didn't realize that it actually was taking much longer than the night before, until Crystal gasped.

"Do you see what time it is?"

"No," I yawned, looking at my watch. "Oh man, four?"

"I have a class in a few hours," she said, as she started to gather her things.

"Yeah, I have to go in to watch film today," I yawned again. "I'll take you home."

"No, you get some sleep. I can catch a cab."

"That's not going to hurt the budget?" I chuckled.

"Nope, I can borrow it from the date emergency fund. Plenty of money there," she laughed.

"Can I ask? Is that because you go on so many great dates or because you don't go on many dates at all?"

"Because I don't date," she shrugged.

"I find that a little hard to believe. Guys must be knocking your door down. "

"I don't have time for that. I'm focused right now. I don't want the distraction. I figure if he's out there, than he'll wait until it's the right time. I won't miss him."

"I see," I answered. "Are you sure I can't take you or maybe you want to sleep here and I can take you to class?"

"*Right*, I'm going to show up to class in the same clothes as yesterday, getting out of your car," she snorted. "No, thanks."

"So what about later? What time do you want to meet?"

"Oh, I have plans. You should enjoy your weekend. I'll see you in class on Tuesday."

"Okay, well, let me walk you down to catch a cab."

"If you insist."

I was a little disappointed that we wouldn't be meeting. I'd gotten used to seeing her so often. I tamped those feelings down and got to my feet, watching as she gathered the last of her things.

I walked her down and hailed her a cab. She waved goodbye, as she got in her cab to leave. With her safely in the car I turned to head back upstairs, musing on the girl that had done a three sixty in personality.

When I got back into my place, I threw myself across the bed. I was out the moment my face touched the sheets. All thoughts of anything forgotten.

CHAPTER THREE

360

I could barely hold my eyes open for the first round of films. I was glad for the break and a minute to breathe. My teammates were laughing, while talking about a party the night before. They had texted me to come out, but I was busy with Crystal and the research project.

"Johnson, what happened last night?" Sean asked.

"I had to handle some schoolwork," I replied.

"Oh yeah, I forgot about that, Bookworm," he chuckled. "You missed it, man. Honey with the green eyes was looking for you."

"Oh yeah?"

"Yeah man. I know you want to know what that right there be like."

Before I could answer him back, my phone began to vibrate. I looked at the caller ID to see it was Crystal. I still had some time to talk so I picked up, before she hung up the line.

"Hello."

"Hey Lee, it's Crystal," she called into the phone.

"What's up?"

"I'm sorry to bother you, but I think I left my organizer at your place. I can't find it and I know that was the last place I remember having it."

"Oh, well, I won't be home for a few hours, but I can let you know if it's there," I said, as I tried to remember if I saw it this morning. My head was banging from trying to think that far back without enough sleep.

"Please, my life is in there."

"No problem. I'll call as soon as I get home."

"Thanks so much, Lee."

"It's cool, Crystal. Talk to you later."

I hung up the phone to Sean shaking his head at me. Sean is one of the veteran players. He always had something to say or an opinion to give. I was sure this time would be no different.

"So Crystal, that's the reason you haven't been coming out?" Sean asked.

"Man, that's my research partner."

"Research partner? I wonder if my wife would go for that one?" Corey laughed.

"Well, you do still remember poker night is at your place?" Brantley asked.

"Yeah, we still on."

The interruption to get back to films was welcomed. I was too tired to think or talk. I just wanted to focus on the films and relax my mind. I made it through the rest of the afternoon, without falling asleep.

I wanted to let Crystal know about her organizer as soon as possible, but I had to stop at the store to get some things for poker night. I did a little shopping and met the guys at my condo. As soon as I opened the door and we walked in, I could see the organizer in between the couch cushions. I placed the bags in the kitchen, taking out my phone to call Crystal.

"Hey Lee, please tell me you found it," she sighed into the phone.

"Yeah, I have it."

"Oh great!"

"Would you like me to bring it to you?" I asked.

"Oh no rookie, you're not bailing out on us," Sean yelled, his laugh booming through my place.

"Oh, it sounds like you're busy. Would it be okay if I come and get it? I won't interfere with your night I don't even have to come in."

"It's cool, you can come. Actually, you can hang out if you want," I offered hoping she would want to.

"Oh, well, it's kind of girl's night out," she replied.

"Well, it's guy's night out here. So your friends are welcome."

"I don't know…I have to think about that one. Would it be okay if I come in like an hour or two?"

"Sure, I'll be here."

"Thanks, see you then," she said, before hanging up.

I hung up and went to put the things in the kitchen away. The guys were making themselves at home, setting up the table. My mind turned to how much I enjoyed last night with Crystal.

I couldn't help hoping she would have a change of heart and decide to hang out.

"Please tell me you didn't just invite some women here," Corey sighed. "My wife will kill me."

"I told you before you wouldn't have to worry about that if you stop hanging with us unmarried men," Sean teased.

"It's just my research partner and some of her friends. I don't think they're going to stay. I don't think she's too into me," I replied.

I'd been thinking out loud. Crystal seemed to stop being so cold to me, but she still wasn't interested. I think she just sees me as a research partner, maybe a friend or someone cool to study with.

"Whatever, Lee, you're an NFL quarterback. Every woman is into you," Sean chuckled.

Two hours went by, before I heard the doorbell. I got up to answer the door hoping once again that Crystal brought her friends and would stay. I opened the door and to my surprise, Crystal and four of her friends were on the other side dressed up like they were going out to the club. Crystal looked great. She had on a pair of tight white jeans, with a white fitted stretch top, a yellow leather jacket, and a pair of yellow platform pumps. I stared at her so hard, I almost forgot to let them in.

"Hey ladies, please come in," I finally managed.

"Hey Lee," Crystal chimed, as she walked in.

Her girlfriends all followed her, waving at me as they passed. Each one of them fine as can be. I gestured for them to have a seat in the living room, where Crystal went to retrieve her organizer off the coffee table where I had placed it.

"Thank you so much," she beamed.

"No problem," I said with a big smile. "Let me introduce you guys to my friends. This is Corey, Paul, Brantley and Sean."

"Hello, ladies," Sean called.

"Hello," they said in unison.

"I'm Crystal, these are my friends Nichelle, Karen, Melissa, and Kelly," she said, as she pointed to each of her friends.

"So are you guys going to hang?" I asked, as I watched Crystal remain standing, while her friends all claimed seats.

"I don't know," Crystal paused, looking at her friends. "We had plans."

"We can stay a while," Melissa interrupted.

"That's what's up," Sean crooned. "Crystal, why don't you come sit on my lap and let me show you how to play poker."

"*Ew*. No, that's okay. I'm good. Thank you," Crystal snorted.

There was something different about her, but I couldn't put my finger on it.

"Would you like to play?" I laughed.

"Sure."

I walked over to the table to my seat, waving her over. She removed her jacket, handing it to her friend Kelly. She paused to bite her lip, a pensive look crossing her face for a minute. Then, she walked over. I held out my hand to offer her my seat. Crystal looked at me shyly, moving over next to me.

"I thought you were going to offer me your lap," she lifted on her toes and said softly into my ear.

I was stunned for a moment. I looked her in the eyes, as she smiled back at me. I let my eyes scan her body again. Reclaiming my seat, I winked at her. Her smile widened and she stepped in between my legs to sit on my lap. I slid us closer to the table, tapping the hand of cards in front of us for her to pick up.

She picked up the cards, while I examined her sitting on my lap. Crystal was a very shapely young woman. I had more than a lap full. She pulled the cards to her chest, leaning into mine to show them to me.

"Which one of you ladies wants to come sit on my lap," Sean called.

Karen jumped up and came over to the table. Another very pretty girl with a cute shape, but she was sort of thin for Sean's taste. I could see in his face she wasn't the one he'd hoped would respond, but she was willing therefore he was taking.

He wasn't the only one taking. After the rest of the ladies came over and sat on barstools around the game, Crystal and I went to town. We snatched everyone's money. After the first three hands, I still remained cautious not to touch her or move wrong. I wanted her to stay right where she was.

"Relax," Crystal leaned back to whisper in my ear.

I reached to place my hand on her waist, as I watched her eyes. She looked back at me, the looks and vibes she was sending my way not at all what I was expecting. She took me by surprise with each minute that passed. When I placed my other hand on her waist, she leaned into my chest and nestled there as we played. We were all having a good time. Sean knows how to keep a room laughing.

After a while, Crystal asked to use the bathroom. I pointed up the hall toward where she could find it, before sliding my chair back to let her rise. I watched as she walked down the hall and could feel my breath squeeze at the sight of her bouncing down the hallway. We waited for her to return, before we continued the game. I made sure everyone was okay on food and drinks while we waited.

When Crystal returned, she came right back to sit on my lap. Only this time, she went to switch sides, which sent me into a bit of a panic. To say I wasn't affected by her sitting in my lap the entire time would be a lie, which in a matter of seconds she wouldn't be able to deny as well. Switching her position lined her up with a big surprise as soon as she sat down.

I knew the moment she felt it. She turned to look me in the face, a smile on her lips. I was truly embarrassed, hoping she didn't say or do anything to let the others know of my situation.

"Do you want me to get up?" she whispered in my ear.

"No, not if you don't want to. You're fine right there," I breathed in her ear.

"Okay, I'm good," she said, winking at me and letting her full ass settle against the heat pulsing beneath her.

I placed a hand on her waist again, the other on her thigh. She didn't seem to mind that either. I wondered what made her so relaxed and laid back that night, but I really didn't care. I liked this girl, a lot. We continued the game, also continuing to take everyone's money, until they all reached their thresholds for the night.

When the game was over, I expected Crystal to get up and sit with her friends, but she didn't move. She propped her elbows on the table, while listening and adding to the conversation. I sat staring at her the entire time. My mind started contemplating what I needed to do to get her to stay with me and let her friends go home.

"Lee, may I use your bathroom?" Karen asked.

"Sure."

"Oh, I'll show you where it is. I have to go again," Crystal chimed.

I slid my seat back again, allowing her room to rise. I watched her get up and walk away. Karen whispered something to her, causing Crystal to turn and catch me watching her.

While holding Karen's hand, she backed her way down the hallway with a smile on her face, as I watched, smiling back at her. The front view was just as nice as the back, I seriously didn't mind which way she walked. Once they disappeared down the hall, I knew I needed to collect myself.

Everyone else moved to the living room to turn up the music and spread out to talk. I made my way into the kitchen to get a glass of water. I stood at the sink, trying to think of anything but Crystal. I started to run plays in my head, which helped a lot. Just as I collected myself and gained some type of focus, I felt small hands wrap around my chest.

"Hey," Crystal called over my shoulder.

I turned to face her.

"Hey," I breathed back at her.

She looked in my eyes and slowly leaned toward me. I felt the pull towards her, leaning back in her direction. We were like magnets, being drawn together. She lifted on her toes, her full lips meeting mine. I was gone.

Crystal had me right there at that moment. I placed my hands on her waist, pulling her to me. She wrapped her arms around my neck, deepening the kiss as she tried to rise higher.

The woman had a talented mouth. Her kisses were amazing. I don't remember how my hands moved to squeeze her plump ass, pulling her closer to me, but they did. She moaned as my grip tightened, pulling a moan from me in response. I groaned when her sexy ass sucked my bottom lip into her mouth. I wanted to squeeze more, pull her closer, but someone clearing their throat drew my attention.

I released Crystal, allowing her to slowly back away. Her movement had absolutely no hush to it, her eyes not peeling from me as her entire face lit up. I finally broke eye contact with her to see who had interrupted. I turned to see it was one of her friends, Nichelle.

"I think maybe it's time to go," Nichelle said, with concern in her voice.

Crystal licked her lips, while still staring at me, a laugh slipping free. "Maybe." She moved back into me, kissing me softly on the lips. "Thanks, I had fun. I'll see you later."

"See you later."

Her friends were lining up at the door. Nichelle stood there waiting for her, holding Crystal's jacket. I walked her to the door to see them out. Crystal kept looking back at me, as they made their way out of the door. I noticed her friends pulling her along. My mind questioned what that was all about. She seemed like she wanted to stay. I would've told my friends to leave if she did.

Once they were gone and the door was closed, I walked over to the couch, flopping down between Sean and Corey. I threw my head back on the cushion and released a long sigh. Crystal was the total package, everything I wanted. I reached up to touch my lips and laughed.

"She's the one," I thought out loud.

"Son, you're not serious?" Sean bellowed. "Man, you need to watch these chicks. She gave you a little kiss and you ready to wife her. These girls are about the money."

"Man, she ain't even know I played until yesterday. Not pro."

"Okay, you said earlier, she wasn't into you?" he reminded me. "Maybe you being pro is what helped change her mind."

"Nah, man, she's not like that. Shorty is ambitious she takes care of herself, she isn't into that bird shit," I explained, but what Sean said did start to register with me.

Crystal's behavior tonight was a lot different than usual.

"Man, it's the smart ones you have to be careful with. That one there is smart and beautiful. Definitely need to watch her," Sean warned.

"I hear that," Brantley chimed in. "Ask my babies' mamas."

"Man, Lee, don't listen to them. I think honey is cool," Corey said, shaking his head.

"Yo, Lee, you goin' to listen to Corey? He's running from his wife," Sean laughed. "What you need to do is holla at shorty with the eyes. Have a good time and forget about trying to wife, Miss. Bookworm."

"Well, I'm calling it a night fellas," Corey announced.

"I bet you are. The Mrs. is blowing that phone up," Sean teased.

"Yeah, well, I'm about to be out too," Brantley laughed. "Crystal's little friend, Melissa, wants to hook up."

"*Oh!*" Corey cheered and gave Brantley five. "My man is on his game, fellas."

I laughed at my teammates as they started to get their things and leave. I had a lot on my mind by the time they left. Sean had a point. Crystal hadn't paid me any attention before that night. I wasn't even sure she liked me. Yet, she was more than willing to be involved this visit. She said the night before she wasn't into dating because she was focused. Which got me to wondering what happened? Man, I didn't want to put her in the category with the gold diggers and groupies. I really liked her.

That still didn't change the facts. She went from ice cold to red-hot overnight. Sean had a point, she's smart. If she wanted to play games, she would definitely know how. I have to be smart and protect myself. I'm a young quarterback, with a great contract. How do I know she didn't know who I was from the beginning? She could've just been pretending she didn't want to be my partner so I would chase her. These women are smart. I'm young, maybe I should stick to having fun for a while.

One thing was for sure, I was going to clear all of this out of my head for the game this weekend. I didn't have time to worry about Crystal or any other groupie. I needed to be focused. My mother was coming down from Connecticut for the weekend and I would make her the only woman I thought about for the next three days. She was the one I knew I could trust.

CHAPTER FOUR

Tipsy Behavior

My weekend went great, I spent some real quality time with my mother and got focused on my goals. Most of all, I had a great game. I not only started, but we won. I was all over the papers.

Having my mother there helped me to stay grounded Monday morning when the calls started and the paper came. I was extremely grateful for that. My mom always reminded me where I came from and all the work it took to get me to where I was. She also helped me see that I hadn't done all I set out to, so there wasn't time to get comfortable.

In the end, I decided to let ideas of Crystal go. I don't need that kind of distraction, as she would say. She was my research partner and I needed to focus on getting my research project done and finishing my degree. Not trying to get with her.

I sat in my usual seat, during class on Tuesday. My plan was to act like nothing happened and keep it moving. That plan fell apart the minute Crystal walked into class. She didn't even look at me. She went right to her seat and took out her books.

I watched her curiously, wondering what was up with her. I think we were the only group not sitting in the same proximity. I was frustrated the whole class. I took my notes and watched her out of the corner of my eye. She never even looked my way.

After class, she collected her things and I decided to beat her out of class to wait. I stood outside where I knew she would pass and I would run into her. She came out of the class and walked right passed me, as she looked down at her phone. I jogged to catch up to her.

"Crystal, you have a minute?" I asked.

She looked up, startled, giving me a weak smile.

"Hey Lee, listen I wanted to talk to you. I'm going to ask the professor to change my partner. You can keep all the research we've done and the topic," she said nervously. "I want to apologize about the other night. I was so uptight about the organizer and my friends thought getting me to drink tequila would help. I didn't mean to complicate things between us."

I stood shocked. I didn't want a new research partner, she was working out fine. We were working well together. I knew something was different the other night. What she said made it all make sense.

"Crystal, about the other night. Let's forget it happened. I don't want to get a new partner. We have so much done. I don't think that would be fair to either of us if we changed now."

She searched my face, with a nervous look in her eyes. "I'm so embarrassed. Lee… I never do things like that. I don't know what I was thinking," she stammered softly.

"It's cool, Crystal. I can separate the two. This is about our project and getting a good grade. The other night was something else. No need to be embarrassed."

"Are you sure this will be okay?" she asked coyly.

"Positive," I assured her. "So I have an away game this weekend, but I leave Thursday night. I thought maybe we could work on the survey and have it ready. That way I can take you to meet my boy at his shop, before I go. You can get started on the sampling this weekend if you want."

"Okay, my class for tomorrow night was cancelled. If you want to meet up to work on the survey after your practice that would be cool. We can go to the shop too, unless you have time before you leave Thursday."

"Actually, I will be free after four tomorrow. We can work on the survey and I'll take you to Kenny's on Thursday," I replied.

"Okay, so I owe you dinner. When was the last time you had a real home cooked meal?" she asked, while smiling up at me.

"What you mean? My chef cooks all the time," I chuckled.

"No, I mean some fried chicken, cornbread, rice and peas and some steamed vegetables?"

"Man, my mom stopped that when I got the chef," I laughed. "You throw down like that?"

"You'll see," Her face beamed. "Is it okay to work at your place?"

"Sure."

"Okay, I'll see you at five. Is that good?"

"Perfect, five at my place."

"Goodnight, Lee."

"Goodnight, Crystal."

I watched her turn and walk away. I couldn't help thinking to myself how wrong Sean could be. Being next to Crystal once again made it hard to put her in that gold digger lane. She had class I didn't see in other women. I thought the way she behaved the other night was something only her man would know about her. I was just lucky to see that side of her for the little while I did.

I walked to my car and drove home. I needed to be alert for practice in the morning. I also wanted to make some notes for the survey and email them to Crystal before we met the next day. When I got home, I took some time to clean up and took a shower. I used that time to get all my mixed up thoughts of Crystal out of my head.

I kept thinking how too good to be true Crystal seemed. Then, it hit me. It dawned on me that she wasn't interested after all. She wanted to change partners to keep from being involved with me. All this thought I'd been giving her was unnecessary.

I got myself together, made my notes, and went to bed. My goals needed to be focusing on starting, winning games, and passing my classes. I fell asleep running the playbook in my head.

CHAPTER FIVE

Conflicted

The next morning, I shined in practice again. I decided to stay late after to workout a little extra. Besides, I had a three o'clock meeting and I needed to kill some time until then. The extra workout time had me focused and ready to handle things ahead of me. My meeting went great. I landed two endorsement contracts, which put me in a real mood to celebrate. I was kind of glad Crystal would be coming over to cook for me.

When I got home, I still had time to shower and change, before Crystal arrived. I threw on a pair of blue jeans and a white button down. I had just finished getting dressed when she arrived, ringing the doorbell. I checked the mirror and ran for the front door.

I opened the door to find her with her hands full. She had her purse, school bag, and grocery bags in her hands. I reached for some of the bags to help her out, as she came through the door.

"Hey Lee, thanks," she sang, as she walked in.

"What's up, Crystal?"

"Am I late?"

"No, you're cool."

"Okay," she breathed. "Today has been a little crazy."

This time I had the pleasure of a friendly smile from her lips. She looked gorgeous as always. A purple cable knit sweater hung off of one shoulder, paired with fitted black slacks. The sweater hid her curves a little, but everything about her remained attractive and appealing to the eye.

I've noticed that her hair is always intact. That's one of the things I like about her, she's always well put together. Most girls that live on campus show up to class in pajama pants and school sweatshirts. I've never seen her look like that.

I placed the grocery bags in the kitchen for her, turning to see her pulling off her sweater, revealing a black thin strapped tank top. Her face looked focused, as she moved, but she still had a light smile on her face. She set up her laptop on the bar and waved me over.

"I figured I can cook and you can work," she said, as she smiled up at me. "I have this great survey software. I saw your notes they were great. We can take those and make a survey super easy."

"Oh, that's what's up!"

"Here, look through it. I want to get started in the kitchen."

She went straight into the kitchen, washing her hands and got to work. I didn't have to tell her where anything was. She moved around the kitchen like a pro, finding everything she needed that she didn't already bring with her.

She started the rice and peas, before mixing the cornbread and popping it in the oven. As that was cooking, she started on the steamed vegetables. She moved quickly, seasoning things up and moving to the next dish.

I tried to work, while sneaking to watch her. The software she had was great. I already had a sample survey in the makings. It was pretty much doing the work for me, as I filled in the questions it asked.

As she washed the chicken and warmed the grease to fry it, she looked over at me. She pulled the cornbread out of the oven, looking just the way I love it. Not too light, not too dark, just perfect. Once she had the chicken breast fried up, she came over to me to see what I had done.

You couldn't miss the energy that swirled through us. It was like electricity sparked through the air, as her fresh scent engulfed me. It was undeniable.

I watched her, as she leaned over the laptop, scanning my work. I know we said we would keep things separate, but I wanted to kiss her again. I wanted to know if it was just the alcohol the other night or did she have interest in me. I wanted to get to know her more.

She turned to ask me a question and without thinking, I reached for her face and kissed her. She didn't resist. She turned her whole body to face me, placing her arms around my neck. I wrapped my arms around her waist, pulling her in close. Crystal kissed even better when she wasn't drunk.

I could feel something between us. The corners of my mouth turned up into a smile as I kissed her. I let my arms close in to hug her tighter.

"Wait, Lee," she pulled away shaking her head. "I thought we were going to separate the two?"

"I am. I like you, Crystal. I want to get to know you," I panted.

"I like you too, but I don't think I'm ready for something like this," she said softly. "Lee, I really need to stay focused. If we try to get to know each other, than I want to move a little slower."

"So, that's not a no?"

"No, it's not a no," she said and frowned. "I knew this was a bad idea."

"Why?"

"I don't know. You just seem like the distraction I've been trying to avoid, but now I can't."

She turned to go into the kitchen to finish up the food and placed it on plates while I thought about her words. She wasn't saying, no. She was saying she wanted to slow down. I figured I could handle that. As long as she was willing to give me a chance, I was willing to slow down. I didn't see how I could be a distraction, we wanted similar things. I felt more like she was the missing piece to my puzzle.

Crystal took the plates over to the table and sat them down, the food smelled and looked great. I walked over to the table to pull out her chair. She smiled, sitting down gracefully.

"Do you want to work while we eat?" she asked.

"No, let's eat. I think I have the survey under control," I replied.

I blessed the table, before we started to tuck in. A groan slipped from my lips as the flavors burst in my mouth. This woman is the one, I know she is. I looked up to see her smiling at me while I inhaled her cooking. I smiled back, trying to finish chewing so I could speak.

"You like?" she asked.

I nodded and cleared my throat. "This is off the hook."

"Thanks," she giggled. "So we're going to the shop tomorrow?"

"Yeah, Kenny will be waiting for us. I can pick you up from your dorm around two."

"Actually, I'll be at the library," she said. "I'm going home this weekend so I need to get some things done. Most likely, I'll do the surveys on Saturday and if I can find time I'll go on Friday."

"Okay, cool. I'll pick you up from the library."

We talked some more about my family while we ate. The subject turning to my dad, I frowned down into my plate.

"He was never really around unless he wanted something from my mom," I said.

"That must have been hard," she replied softly.

I shrugged.

"I'm good. I don't really get too involved with him. He's a character. He has never truly supported me in anything. He's always about some drama. I can do without it. Besides, I have done fine without him."

"You seem to have good friends," she changed subjects with a smile on her face.

"Yeah, Kenny is the closest thing I have to a brother. Him and Kim are the ones who helped my mom keep me grounded," I nodded.

I started to ask her about her family, but my cell rang. I went over to the counter to pick it up, seeing it was Sean. I should've known he would be calling tonight. I'm sure the word on my new contracts had gotten out.

"What's up, man?" I answered the phone.

"Yo, I know you coming out tonight," Sean called into the phone.

"I don't know, man. I'm a little busy tonight."

"Please tell me you not trippin' over there, over that bookworm. You better watch that man, can't trust a big butt and a smile. Besides, I think shorty is coming out tonight. You need to get with that," Sean coached into the phone.

I stopped to think. Crystal did have my mind some place she wasn't ready to go. I have to admit, I did want to move a little faster with her. On the other hand, little mama from the club has been giving me the eye for a minute. However, Crystal was what I really wanted. I could feel the conflict tugging within me. It was a battle between what my body wanted and what my mind knew I needed. As if reading my inner debate Crystal spoke up, pushing the decision in my body's favor.

"Lee if you have something to do, I can finish the survey up," she whispered.

"Come on, Lee. Don't miss out on tonight. You should be celebrating," Sean encouraged.

I looked at Crystal, warring just a little more. I did deserve to celebrate. Besides, she was giving me an out.

"Alright, Sean, I'll meet you in two hours," I sighed.

Crystal started to pick up our plates, making her way into the kitchen to clean up. I followed to help her. Secretly wishing she would change her mind. I would love to stay home with her. All she had to do was say the word, I would completely forget about everything else.

"Lee, do you have something I can put this in?" she asked.

"You can put those pots right in the refrigerator like that. I'mma finish that off when I come back," I said as I smiled at her, while I rubbed my stomach.

"You're a mess," she giggled.

She packed up her laptop, once she was done in the kitchen and put on her sweater. I walked over to her to see if maybe she would give me a reason not to go to the club. She looked up at me with a smile, as she searched my face.

"I'll see you tomorrow at two," she said before turning to leave.

I was very disappointed. I let her out, before proceeding to go get dressed to go out. I didn't know what to think about Crystal. I didn't think Sean was right about her, but I planned to find out what made her tick.

When Sean and I arrived at the club, and sure enough the chick with the eyes was there. Her face lit up the moment she saw me. She looked good too. With her shoulder length reddish brown hair and her caramel skin, she had on this extra tight black dress that showed off her cute little body. Crystal is better looking if you did the math, but little mama was no joke herself.

I walked over to her and started a conversation. Soon I had the drinks coming her way and kept them flowing throughout the night. She giggled and whispered in my ear, trying to act all cute. I had already made up my mind, I was taking her home. She didn't have to try so hard, it was a done deal.

After about two hours, I threw Sean the peace sign, leading shorty out by the small of her back. I saw the excitement light up her eyes when my car pulled up and I opened the door for her. It was a bit of a turn off, as my mind turned to Crystal's lack of reaction. I frowned, but shrugged it off and got in the car.

CHAPTER SIX

Friends

I woke up the next morning to the smoke alarm going off in my condo. I jumped up out of the bed and ran to the kitchen. Rachael from last night stood in the kitchen in one of my jerseys, fanning at some burnt eggs.

How do you burn eggs? I thought to myself, shaking the rest of the fog from my head. I had to still be sleeping. No one burns eggs.

"Oh sorry, baby, I was trying to make you breakfast," Rachael said, turning to me with a shamed look on her face.

"Look, Ma, I need to get to practice. Why don't you go get dressed," I replied, trying not to sound annoyed.

"Oh, okay."

I cleaned up in the kitchen, before going to get ready for practice. When I stepped out of the bathroom, Rachael had my cell phone in her hands programming her number into it. I scowled at her when her phone started to ring telling me she just called herself from my phone.

I was a little annoyed. Last night was kind of a disappointment. I would have to remember to never judge a book by its cover. She was definitely a book that could've stayed on the shelf.

"Let's go," I grumbled once dressed and ready to go.

I remained pretty much silent after that. I dropped her at the train station and made my way to practice. Guilt and something else riding me as I questioned the night before.

Sean wanted to know all about my night. Even if I was the type of guy to tell, it wasn't worth talking about. I shrugged it off and changed the subject. In my mind, I knew I wanted to see Crystal, no one else compared to her and I think last night proved it—even if I've never slept with her, I just knew.

When I got to campus, Crystal was out in front of the library waiting. She looked extra good, with a pair of tight dark blue jeans and these black boots that came up over her knees. A pink leather jacket draped over her arm, while the pink top she had on clung to her in the right places, hanging off of one shoulder like her sweater from the day before.

That look works for her, I thought licking my lips.

She climbed into the car, before I could get out to open her door. I could smell her perfume take over the confined space, not in an overwhelming way but in a sweet heady way that tightened my groin and my stomach. I couldn't help myself, I leaned over to her pecking her on the cheek. She looked too cute not to.

"Hey, Lee," she giggled.

"Hey, Crystal," I said. "I was thinking, would you like to use my car this weekend to go back and forth to the shop?"

"No, Lee," she laughed. "I'm good on transportation."

"Okay, just trying to help the budget."

"Thanks for looking out," she beamed. "I finished the surveys and consent forms last night. I had them printed up this morning. You can look them over before you leave."

"Great."

"How has your day been? How was practice?" she asked getting comfortable in her seat.

Her interest in my day hit me in the chest. I like the fact that she puts me on display and shows interest in what I want. I talked most of the way to the shop, but I wanted to hear more about her.

"So how was your day?" I asked, once I wrapped up what was going on with me.

"Interesting, my mother has been text messaging me all day, driving me crazy about the big graduation party she's throwing," she chuckled. "She wants to know if I have a date yet."

"Well, do you?"

She looked at me and rolled her eyes.

"Please, Lee. I don't have time to chase guys around, asking them to come to the ridiculous gala my mother insists on throwing."

"Well, you don't have to chase me. Just ask," I chuckled.

"You're probably busy," she said softly.

"You don't know if you don't ask. Let me know the date, I'll check my schedule," I offered, as we pulled up in front of the shop.

"Thanks," she leaned and kissed me on the cheek. "I'll text you the information later."

I cut off the car and turned to face her. Her lips were shiny and sparkling, just inviting me in. I tilted my head and lean toward her. She leaned in, kissing me just as I yearned for. After a little while, she pulled away with a big grin on her face.

"You're trouble. I want to tell you no, but I can't help saying, yes," she breathed.

I chuckled, getting out to open the door for her. When she stepped out of the car, all the guys in front of the shop stopped to stare. Seeing me in the Porsche was getting old, but seeing Crystal was definitely something new. We walked into the shop and Kenny's voice was the first thing I heard.

"*Oh*, it's the star," Kenny called out. "What's up, my man?"

"What's up, Kenny?" I grinned. "I want to introduce you to my research partner, Crystal."

"Well, hello, Crystal. If I go back to college, do I get one too," he teased.

"Hi, it's nice to meet you," Crystal said, holding out her hand with a laugh.

"How are you doing?" Kim asked as she came over.

"Hi, I'm fine," Crystal replied, holding her hand out to her as well.

"Crystal, this is Kim. Kenny's sister and the co-owner."

"Oh, it's nice to meet you. Lee said a lot of nice things about you guys."

"He better," Kim smiled. "Ma, that cut is banging. You need to let me put some color to it and you'll really have these fools out here drooling."

"She don't need nothing else to get nobody drooling, mommy popping just like that," Kenny crooned.

"Come, Crystal. I want to introduce you to the girls. I already let them know you and Lee were coming," Kim said, as she grabbed Crystal's hand and pulled her to the stylist side of the shop.

I took off my coat, sitting in the vacant barber chair next to Kenny. He was supposed to be finishing a cut, but his eyes were watching Crystal. I snorted and cleared my throat at him. He turned to look at me with a grin.

"Wow, she's bad," Kenny said, low enough for me to hear.

"Yeah, I know."

"Word, son, if you not trying to holla at her, let me know."

"Kenny, you trippin'," I shook my head at him laughing.

"Whatever."

I watched Crystal fall into her element. She talked business with Kim, giving suggestions to better things around the place. She even started schooling the stylist on cutting. I watched, as she took the scissors to show one of the girls how to perfect the cut she'd been attempting.

Crystal is nice with it. I know the girl getting the actual cut and she never looked as good as she did when Crystal was done. I could tell Crystal loves styling hair and teaching.

We must've spent two hours there, while Crystal fell in right at home. By the way Kim kept her in conversation and laughed with her, I could tell Kim liked Crystal. It was something to watch because Kim doesn't just take well to everyone.

Crystal looked at her watch, as she explained a technique to one of the girls. A few minutes later, she came over to where Kenny and I were. I smiled at her, as she approached with a warm smile in return.

"So Kenny, I'll be back Saturday and I may try tomorrow," Crystal said.

"Baby, you can come here anytime. Day or night," he crooned.

"Thanks," she giggled. "Lee, I have to go. I have to head home to meet my mom."

"No problem, I need to get ready for my flight."

We got in the car and I drove her back to campus. On the way, we talked about Kenny and Kim's place. It's a great shop and location.

"A while back they had asked me to come in on the business with them but I never made up my mind," I told her.

"I have all types of ideas for that place to triple their income," she chimed enthusiastically.

I believed her, I was sure she could. I kept sneaking peeks at her as she animatedly threw out some of her ideas. They were good, really good actually.

I have to admit, I was upset when we made it to campus and she had to go. I would miss her this weekend. Once again, she had my thoughts somewhere she wasn't willing to go. Just looking at her sent blood pumping through my veins.

"Have a safe trip and good luck with the game," she said softly, as she went to step out of the car.

"I'll call you when I get back," I replied.

She paused, turning back to face me.

"Okay," she said, looking at me for a minute, before leaning in to kiss me on the cheek. "Later, Lee."

I drove off, wishing I had more time with her. I know I needed to get her off my mind for this weekend. Worrying about making her my girlfriend was only a recipe for trouble. As I tried to clear my head and focus, my phone rang. I picked up, not bothering to check the caller Id.

"Hello," I answered.

"Hey, baby," I heard Rachael's voice spill through the line. I wasn't expecting her to call so soon. "Listen, I wanted to see you."

"Ma, I got a plane to catch," I answered.

"Oh, well, maybe when you come back," she said in a seductive tone.

"Maybe, I need to go."

"Okay, I'll call you later."

I hung up the line, before she said another word. She was certainly not what I needed in that moment. I had my head in the game ready to go.

CHAPTER SEVEN

Mistake

I couldn't wait for class Tuesday night. Sean had been trying to make my life miserable, giving me lecture on top of lecture about why Crystal wasn't the one. He felt I should've been out partying more during the away game. I wasn't interested and not just because of Crystal.

I was focused. I didn't have time for all the interruptions and distractions. I needed to keep my head.

When Tuesday did roll around, I sat in class waiting for Crystal to walk in. We talked earlier for a brief minute. She had gotten a few of the surveys completed, but it sounded like she had more fun hanging out in the shop.

When she walked into class I couldn't help the huge grin that stretched across my face. The knee length denim dress and stiletto leather boots where on point. Instead of going to her usual seat, she came to my row taking a seat next to me. To my surprise she leaned over, kissing me on the cheek but I wasn't about to complain.

"Hey, my little brother was going on and on about the game. I hear you did really good. Congratulations," she sang.

"Thanks."

"Here are the copies of the finished surveys. There are twenty so far."

"Okay, you want to go back this week, we can start on Thursday?"

"Okay, but I'll have to meet you there. My mom needs me to come home Thursday morning."

"Oh okay," I replied.

The professor called class to order and Crystal shut me off. All of her attention turned to class. I laughed to myself. Crystal reminded me of myself at game time. I get the same way. I don't think she remembered I was in the room until class was dismissed.

"You still want to go to dinner?" I asked as she packed her things.

"Lee, can I be honest?"

"Sure, what's good?"

"I'm too tired to sit in a restaurant tonight," she replied.

"Oh, okay so maybe another time."

I know I wasn't hiding my disappointment. I'd been looking forward to spending time with her.

"I didn't say I was too tired for you," she smiled. "I just thought maybe we could do take out or something. I can come to your place."

I liked her idea. I didn't mind some alone time with her. My thoughts must have crossed my face, because she raised a brow at me.

"That's cool with me," I said with a grin.

"I bet it is," she laughed. "Lee, I still have my taser and my emergency date fund."

"I thought we were passed all that," I retorted.

"I don't know. I don't like that look in your eyes," she giggled.

"Come on, I'm starving."

We drove to my place, after deciding to order from my favorite pizza place. I took note of how tired she actually looked. She didn't talk as much as usual, only answering my questions. After a while I got quiet and let her rest her eyes.

When we got to my apartment, I needed to answer a call from my agent so I went to my room for a little privacy. While on the phone I straightened up my room. When I was done with both I returned to the living room to find Crystal curled up on the rug with her shoes off.

I went over to her, sitting down next to her. Reaching out, I started to rub circles on her back. She sighed, moving closer to me. It struck me to give her a real massage. I gently placed my other hand on her back kneading it gently.

"I think you're trying to become my best friend," She moaned tiredly. "I so need this. Thank you."

Sitting up she turned her back to me to give me better access.

"No problem. You look tired. Maybe I should've taken you home."

"What and miss this? Your hands feel amazing."

"Oh yeah," I chuckled before reluctantly saying. "I can take you home after we eat if you want."

"Nope, I'm fine. I sort of missed you."

"I missed you too," I breathed in her ear as I wrapped my arms around her, pulling her back into my embrace.

Turning her face toward mine, she reached for the back of my neck. As she stared in my eyes I leaned in to kiss her. It started out nice and soft, a sweet kiss. Until her perfume filled my head, followed by a low sigh.

I reached for her face, adding more passion to the kiss. She moved to turn her body toward mine, raising to her knees to wrap her arms around my neck. I gently grabbed her waist, pulling her into my chest. Both of our breathing increased. Crystal tried to press her body as close as she could get. I'd been just about to pull her into my lap when the doorbell rang.

Just that fast I'd forgotten we were waiting for dinner. I released her to open the door. Once I'd paid for the food, I took the pizza to the table and retrieved plates from the kitchen. I figured I better get her something to eat, not to mention I was hungry myself. I wanted her to stay but if she didn't want to I wanted to at least make sure she ate.

Placing the plates on the table, I watched as she walked towards me. I never noticed how small she was compared to me. We were both without shoes, revealing how much taller than her I truly was. I found it kind of cute.

I pecked her on the lips once she reached me, drawing a smile from her lips. We piled our plates with food, going back into the living room to sit on the couch.

I loved the pinwheels from the pizza place I ordered from. Crystal had never had one, prompting me to talk her into trying mine. I laughed at the look of pleasure on her face when she took her first bite.

I had a feeling it was now on her list of favorites. Noting that for the future reference, I gave her the rest of the pinwheel from my plate. It didn't take long for us to fall into an easy banter.

"How are things coming with your party? Your mother still planning?" I asked.

"Ugh, she's the reason I'm so drained," she groaned.

"A lot to deal with?"

"You would not believe." She huffed, pressing together those sexy lips.

Honestly, she looked exhausted just thinking about it. Her shoulders sagged as she told me a little more about the planning of her party.

"She means well, but she's been driving me crazy the last few days," Crystal frowned, moving to change the subject. "How's your mom?"

"She's good. Keeping me in check as usual," I nodded.

"That's good," she laughed.

We fell into more topics. The comfort level between us growing by the minute. I enjoyed the time I got to spend with her. It was something I never find with anyone else.

"So Lee, did you miss me?" she asked, once our plates were empty before us.

"You have no idea," I said, taking her plate to place it on the coffee table with mine.

"What would your mother think about me?" she quizzed. "I know she must stay on top of you about the women you date."

"I think she would love you." I shrugged.

My mother is extremely laid back. If I like someone she accepts my judgment. Crystal didn't have to worry about that.

"Really? Why is that?"

"I don't know, you're smart, you cook, and you're focused. I think she would feel relieved that she doesn't have to worry about me with you in my life."

"Do you feel that way? Like I'd take care of you?" she asked with a grin on her lips, tilting her head to the side.

I shrugged my shoulders. My eyes searching her pretty face. I have a million and one thoughts about her running through my head.

"I think, I'm still trying to figure that out, but I believe so," I replied.

"Is that what you want?" she asked seductively. "Do you want me to take care of you?"

I moved closer to her and put my hands on her waist. Our connection was undeniable. I could feel it tugging us together.

"I want to take care of you," I breathed in her face, before kissing her lips. "But yeah, I would like if you took care of me too."

She stared up at me, biting her lip. Confusion settled across her face as thoughts turned in her head. I could see the gears turning. I gave her time, not wanting to rush her or make her decide to leave. Little did I know that's exactly where her thoughts were headed.

"Lee, maybe I should go," she murmured.

"Did I say something wrong?"

"No," she said. Discomfort covering her expression as she looked back at me. "You said something right. I like you a lot. I don't trust myself with you. It would just be better if I go."

She stood up to retrieve her boots. I tried to think of something, anything, to say to stop her but nothing came to mind. I was usually a quick thinker in this department but not with Crystal. She made me second-guess everything.

"I'll take you home," I finally responded.

"No, that's okay. I'll take a cab."

"Wow, is it that bad? I'm an emergency date," I teased.

"No," she laughed. "You have practice in the morning, right? I'm taking care of you."

"Well, me making sure you get to campus safely would be taking care of you," I tossed back, wrapping my arms around her.

"Don't worry about it. I'll be safe. You look tired too. I'll just give you a call when I get to the dorm."

"You sure? It's not a problem. I can take you," I reassured her.

"No, I'm good."

"Then I'll pay for the cab."

"No, you won't," she grinned. "You can walk me downstairs though. Give me less time to have to miss you."

My heart danced to the sound of her words. I'd already begun to miss her. Still, I was glad to know she would miss me as well. I started punching holes in my thoughts concerning all the things Sean had been drilling into my head.

Crystal was the first girl to turn down money from me. It didn't feel like she was playing games, but I was so into her I couldn't be sure. I was still a little apprehensive, just in case.

I walked her down to hail her a cab, kissing her good night. When I got back upstairs I cleaned up and got some homework done while I waited for her to call me. I was anxious to know when she arrived at her dorm safely.

I was tired, but I didn't want to lie down and miss her call. I busied myself with some cleaning and mentally running through a few plays we'd be focused on in the morning. Time flew by as I got lost in the mundane tasks before eventually settling in with a textbook.

It didn't take much time for her to get to campus. My phone rang while I fought my way through reading. I picked up, rubbing my eyes.

"Hello," I yawned into the phone.

"Hey baby, what's up? Did I wake you?" Rachael's voice came through the other end.

"Oh, Ma, what's up, look this isn't a good time."

"Lee, when can I see you again?" she asked.

"I don't know about that," I tried to sound polite.

Rachael had been blowing my phone up for days. I would never have given her my number. I was still pissed I left my phone around in the first place.

"Oh…did I do something wrong?"

"I thought we were just kicking it that night. I am kind of focused on the game. I'm not looking for a relationship," I replied.

"But I thought we were having a good time. It doesn't have to be a relationship."

"Yeah, I just don't think this is going to work."

A pause came on the other end. I just wanted to hang up and was seriously considering it. At the same time, my other line started to beep. I knew it was Crystal. I needed to go.

"Listen, like I said this isn't a good time. I've got to go," I said, hanging up to answer Crystal.

"Hello," I called once I switched over.

"Hey, Lee," responded the voice I wanted to hear. "I'm safe and in my room about to pass out in my bed."

"Okay," I chuckled. "Can I call you tomorrow?"

"If you can catch me in between classes, sure," she yawned.

"Alright, cool, goodnight."

"Goodnight."

I hung up and took my butt to bed. I was tired and I would need to be rested in the morning. The coaches wanted to change things up a little. I need to be ready to hold down my spot.

CHAPTER EIGHT

The Last to know

Wednesday was painful. Between my schedule and Crystal's, I barely got to speak to her for five minutes. I didn't realize how busy I would get with my success on the field. It was as if my agent had me on speed dial. Every five minutes he'd call with something new.

Don't get me wrong, I was definitely excited for all the attention and success. The opportunities were amazing for my rookie year. I just didn't realize how fast it would all happen.

Kenny's shop brought me a needed dose of reality. Kenny and Kim always kept it real with me. I wanted their opinion on Crystal, as well as some of the offers coming my way for endorsements.

My mom always gives me good advice. I just hadn't told her about Crystal yet. I wanted to make sure she's the one I want to take home to my mother.

"Lee, you're bugging. Crystal is a good girl. She's what you need to be dealing with and not them birds in the club. You think I haven't been putting my ear to the streets? I know what you been up to," Kim said, as she narrowed her eyes at me.

"Cut me some slack, Kim." I laughed.

"This isn't funny, Lee. I warned you before. That Rachael chick, she's bad news."

"Wow, Kim," I sat up in my seat. I was truly shocked. "You be spying on me like that? I was with her once and I told her I'm not interested."

"Honey, you don't understand. Once is all chicks like her need. I hope you were careful," Kim said, sounding truly concerned.

"Man, I told you before, leave them club birds alone. Crystal is definitely where it's at and she likes your fool behind," Kenny grumbled.

"I don't see you staying away from them club birds," I teased Kenny.

"You don't see me with millions of dollars yet either," Kenny retorted, turning his mouth up at me in a sour frown. "Them girls aren't tryin' to trap me, Son. You on the other hand, my dude, they are."

"Well, what makes you think Crystal isn't trying?" I asked.

Kim burst out laughing. She walked away shaking her head. Kenny frowned at me while he shook his head, going back to focusing on the client before him.

Kenny looked like he wanted to hit me or something. I wanted to know what made them so sure about Crystal. Kenny looked up at me again, repeating the shake of his head.

"Stupid," Kenny said under his breath, shaking his head some more.

I folded my arms across my chest and frowned. Turning, I stared out of the shop window lost in thought. A few minutes ticked by before a purple Maserati pulled up.

My brow lifted in curiosity. Usually I was the only one to pull up in cars that exotic. I laughed, turning to Kenny.

"So you stepping up your clientele," I teased, nodding out the window.

Kenny looked up to see what I was talking about and roared with laughter. He looked at me with a curious gaze, again shook his head. I shrugged my shoulders at him. I was obviously missing something.

"Stupid," Kenny said again, this time loud enough for me to truly hear.

I looked back outside to see Crystal come from around the driver's side of the Maserati. She opened the trunk and pulled out her laptop before making her way into the shop. She looked like a super model in a pair of knee high grey boots and a black flared out mini skirt. A grey knit top finished it all off, hanging from those sexy shoulders just the way I like.

I sat confused and suddenly annoyed. How does a girl with a food budget and emergency date budget have a hundred and twenty something thousand-dollar car? Why didn't I know she had it? Was it because she was a gold digger? Was she that good at what she did?

I would hide something like that if I were playing a role too. I watched her walk into the shop just like all the other guys were. She walked straight over to me, placing a kiss on my cheek. I didn't know how to respond. I sat in stunned silence.

"Hey, Lee," she chimed with a big grin. "Sorry I couldn't get here sooner."

"No problem," I answered. "So which budget is the Maserati in?"

My curiosity got the better of me. I needed to hear the answer to this one. Some things weren't adding up for me.

A puzzled look crossed her face. Her eyes looked deep into mine. A quick laugh left her lips.

"The...I'm a spoiled brat budget." She shrugged and walked away to go talk to Kim.

"Yo, Lee, you about to mess that up, big time," Kenny hissed at me.

"What makes you so sure she's alright Kenny?" I grumbled. "How you know she ain't got some dude or dudes buying her expensive cars?"

It didn't dawn on me until that very moment how nice Crystal truly dressed. Her bags alone should have tipped me off. I know girls that hustle that don't have the types of bags that Crystal has. Her clothes looked more in the price range of the stuff I see other players' wives wear. For example, the boots she was wearing today were clearly high quality and she had a Gucci bag on her arm.

"Son, have you been asking her about her family? Did you even ask her who her father is?" Kenny laughed. "Stupid."

"Yo, man, you got one more of those before I tackle you."

"Yeah, well, you mess this up and you gonna be saying it to yourself," he chuckled.

Crystal came back over, but as hard as I tried, I couldn't get out of my funk. I had too many things going on in my head. Her car, Sean's voice, her change in interest in me, and her talks of budgets—when it was clear she wasn't on one driving a car like that.

"Do you want to get started?" she asked.

"Yeah, you have the surveys?"

"I just realized I left them in the car. I was rushing to see you," her face twisted a little as the words left her mouth. Disappointment surfaced on her pretty face before she spoke her next words. "I'll go get them."

I watched her walk outside. Neil, one of my boys that's always smooth with the ladies walked up to the shop just as she reached her car. He stopped to watch Crystal, following her inside as she returned. Neil stays fly. One look will tell you that he gets his paper. He's a smooth dude, not hood at all when it comes to his game.

I sat back to watch Crystal's reaction to him. Surely if she's about brothers with money she would reveal a lot with a sly talker and shot caller like Neil. At least, that's what I'd told myself.

"Excuse me," Neil called reaching into his pocket to pull out his card.

Crystal frowned but turned to answer.

"My name is Neil," he said, extending the card to her. "I've never seen you here before are you from around here?"

Crystal turned to look at me then mouthed '*help.*' I shrugged my shoulders at her, but remained in the chair I was seated in. Her face became furious. I wasn't sure what I was thinking anymore.

"No," I heard her answer as she turned back, ignoring the card in his outstretched hand.

"You mind telling me your name?" Neil quizzed.

"My name is Crystal, but honey, let me save you some time. I'm not interested. I don't have time for whatever you want. But you have a nice day," she said politely and turned to throw the surveys in my lap before storming past me.

"You don't listen," Kenny sighed. "You mind if I holla, cause you done."

He chuckled, shaking his damn big ass head at me again.

Crystal disappeared into the back office with Kim for hours. I worked on getting the surveys taken care of. Luckily, one of the girls from the shop tried to help. We were there until closing. Plenty of time for me to think about what had happened.

Kenny made it seem like I was missing a key point to all of this. Crystal talked about her family on a few occasions but I can't say it was enough to clue me off to anything out of the ordinary.

I know she goes home to see them, but to be honest, I don't even know where home is. I'm always answering her questions about me. I never got too deep into her life other than the party her mother's planning for her.

Now that I think of it, the place her party is going to be at seems like it's going to be seriously nice. She had texted me the address along with the date so I could see if I could make it. But that didn't mean much. People throw parties at fancy places to show off all the time.

I was so annoyed I couldn't think straight. All I could hear was Sean in my head. I started to get pissed because I'm more than capable of thinking for myself. I should've never let Sean's words creep into my head in the first place.

"Can you copy those and bring them to class next week?" Crystal asked, interrupting my thoughts.

"Yeah," I answered looking down at the surveys I collected. "Can we talk?"

"No, we're done with that," she said curtly. "Let's just get this project done."

Kenny chuckled, shaking that damn head for the millionth time while cleaning to lock the place up. I wanted to throw something at him. Kim tossed me a mean glare, narrowing her eyes at me with her arms across her chest. I knew I was in for it with her.

"So Crystal, I'll meet you at the dorm around ten?" Kim chimed, now ignoring me.

"Yeah, I'll be ready."

"And you know we're taking your car. No way am I showing up in my Corolla if you got a Maserati," Kim teased.

"That's cool," Crystal laughed. "I can take it back to the lot before class in the morning."

"Okay, cool, so I'll see you in a few," Kim sang, hugging Crystal.

"See you. Thanks again Kenny if you want to come out tonight, I can get you in too. Kim will tell you about it I need to go," Crystal said as she walked toward the door. She didn't even look in my direction.

As soon as she walked out of the door Kim popped me in the back of the head. I turned to scowl at her, but found a killer look on her face. I didn't know what she was so mad about, I was the one that just got blown off.

"What's wrong with you?" she hissed.

"Whatever, Kim," I grumbled.

"Don't, whatever me. That girl likes you and you showed your black behind in here today. I don't even know this person sitting here. When you find Lee, tell him I'm looking for him."

"Seriously," Kenny chimed in.

"How y'all just taking her side?" I muttered. "Why I ain't know she riding like that?"

"Kenny, please tell me he didn't just say that," Kim gasped. "This is about her car?"

"Sis, don't even bother. Somebody is getting in his head," Kenny answered. "He thinks she wants him to trick on her."

"Boy, Crystal don't need your money. You got it twisted. Oh well. I don't see the point in explaining now. You done messed that up anyway." Kim shook her head at me and rolled her eyes.

I got up to go for the door. I had enough to think about. I wasn't going to sit here and listen to them.

Crystal was done with me? So be it. I was done trying to figure her out. I would just stick to my project and nothing more when it came to her.

As I got in my car, Sean sent me a text about a party. I was in the mood to release some stress. I was absolutely going out. I rushed home to get ready. I needed to meet Sean in time to get into the club. This was one party my rookie status wasn't going to get me in.

CHAPTER NINE

Get this Right

I showered, putting on a fresh pair of slacks and a black dress shirt. I made sure to get fresh from head to toe. I'm not big on buying crazy jewelry, but I did buy a diamond bracelet and watch. I put them on, on my way out the door.

It took me longer than I thought to get to the club. Sean kept sending me impatient text messages. When I pulled up, he was out front surrounded by a bunch of women. I stepped out of the car and on to the curb to meet him.

"You had like five more seconds and I was going in," Sean taunted.

"Whatever, man," I chuckled. "I'm ready to clear my head."

"Shorty bookworm?"

"Not tonight Sean," I cautioned.

I followed Sean into the club. When we stepped inside, Sean wrapped his arm around the waist of the hostess that led us up to the VIP area. The place was crawling with wall-to-wall freaks checking us out. None that caught my eye though. I wasn't sure why I'd agreed to come out after all.

As we sat at our table I noticed a table across from us. I knew the guy in the center with people surrounding him. I'd met him through some friends. He was a well-known rapper in the area.

His table wasn't just filled with people. They had bottles everywhere. I remembered him because he was a cool dude. I decided to go over and say what's up. I was pretty sure he would remember me.

"Hey, what's up, KG?" I said as I sauntered up to the table.

"Oh, my man, Lee Johnson. What's good?"

"Nothing, man, chillin'," I answered, stepping a little closer.

As I moved in, Kim came into view. I was stunned for a moment. I recalled her and Crystal mentioned getting together.

"Yo, this is my new friend, Kim," KG said with a blinding smile.

"Man, I know Kim. She's like my sister."

"Word? It's a small world," KG replied as he gave me five, pulling me over to his side. "So you probably know my little cousin then. Yo, Derrick, tell Coco, come here. I want her to meet someone."

KG smelled like he'd already taken a few bottles to the face. His speech had even started to alter. Kim wouldn't even look at me but I noticed the smirk on her face.

I looked around quickly to see if I saw Crystal, but I came up short. I only noticed the big bodyguard dude that must have been named Derrick. He was heading back our way with a female wrist in his hand, as he pushed through the crowd to get to us. I knew it was a female wrist because of the fingernails and the diamond tennis bracelet on it.

My mouth almost flew open when Derrick made it to us, stepping out of the way. Crystal stared back at me. When she saw me the smile on her face faded.

She looked amazing. I had never seen her dressed like this. She was wrapped in a black dress that plunged down to her bellybutton and left little to the imagination. That hourglass figure was on full display. The gold platform heels on her feet made her short thick legs look like chocolate candy.

KG patted me on the shoulder, waving Crystal forward to his other side. I was too stunned to move let alone say a word.

"Coco, this is my boy, Lee," KG slurred, "Lee, this is my cousin, Coco."

"I know Lee already. I know you didn't call me over here for him," Crystal said sounding fully annoyed.

"Oh word? Sorry, cuz. Excuse me waitress, please get my moody cuz another drink. She still acting too uptight," KG called out.

I chuckled at that. Crystal was always uptight. I had only seen her relax the few times we were alone together.

She looked at me and frowned. I needed to talk to her. Seeing her tonight reminded me of how much I liked her, how much I wanted her. I was stupid to behave the way I did over the car.

Crystal moved to sit next to Kim, KG retaking his seat. He leaned into Kim's ear on the opposite of Crystal. Whatever he said brought a smile to Kim's lips. I noticed the space beside Crystal.

Flagging down the waitress, I ordered a drink. Smoothly, I strolled over, taking the seat at Crystal's side. She stiffened and shifted all the way towards Kim.

I wasn't deterred. I leaned to whisper in her ear, causing her to become all the more rigid. I sighed before I spoke a word. Throwing caution to the wind, I manned up on my mistake and pushed forward.

"Crystal, I'm sorry about earlier. Can we talk?" I started.

She turned to face me with her eyes narrowed.

"I don't even know what that was earlier," she hissed. "I don't have time for games, Lee. We are done."

"I was trippin' over some bullshit, *I* don't even understand. I just want to talk."

She turned toward the waitress that arrived with her drink, taking it. Her hand shot up in a gesture for another. She downed the drink in her hand, turning her eyes to look at me for a minute. A frown took over her pretty face and she turned away.

The waitress showed up with my drink at the same time as Crystal's second. I watched her finish that one too, before she grabbed Kim to move for the dance floor. I took a sip of my drink and fell back against the seat.

"Don't look like that. Coco don't give nobody no play," KG chuckled. "She's into school. All this rap and athlete shit doesn't faze her. She still not tryin' to hear what dudes out here spitting."

My curiosity goes through the roof. Just so happens KG was drunk enough to tell me anything I wanted to know. I wasn't going to miss out on this opportunity.

As I thought of a plan to pry, I continued to watch Crystal on the dance floor. She sent away guy after guy, not even bothering to give them a second glance.

We were in a VIP full of guys with money. I recognized some of the heavy ballers she was swatting away. None of that seemed to phase her.

"KG, tell me something." I leaned in his direction, still watching Crystal. "Where she get that nice car from?"

"Oh, are you kidding? Coco's daddy's little girl. He buys all them cars," he laughed. "Only thing I ever seen my uncle say no about was paying her tuition. He ain't think she was going to finish. She used to be my partner in crime, until she started school."

He kept calling Crystal, Coco. Something about it rung a distant bell that I couldn't put my finger on. I did, however, understand why Kenny thought I needed to ask her more about her family. Crystal could care less about my money if she was spoiled by her father. I also remembered her saying something about her father not thinking she would finish school. She was doing this degree on her own.

I watched as she turned down another guy that tried to dance up on her. I decided right then and there...I wanted her. I was tired of listening to Sean's raving in my head. This girl was perfect for me in every way. I was the one guy in the club she couldn't say no to.

She'd told me so herself. I chugged down my drink. Standing, I set my sights on the dance floor.

I walked up behind Crystal, placing one hand on her hip. The other, I boldly slid into the opening of her dress to rub my thumb against her smooth stomach. She stiffened at my touch, turning to react to whoever dared to touch her. I quickly pecked the side of her lips, when her face came into view. I could feel as she relaxed when it registered with her it was me. I pulled her body closer to me and started to dance with her.

She turned her entire body to face me, wrapping her arms around my neck. Her orbs searched for something in my eyes. When she found it, she lifted herself up to kiss me. I returned the kiss, not holding back how much I wanted her. A moan slipped from her lips, carrying over the music. Reaching down, I slid my hand up her thigh. My mouth curved into a smile as I devoured hers.

"Come home with me," I pulled away to whisper in her ear.

She stood staring up at me. I could see the no in her eyes, but I felt the yes on her lips. She had to say yes. From that fire kiss, I knew she wanted me as much as I wanted her.

"Crystal, I want to take you home with me." I said after her lack of response.

"Okay," she said softly.

"Let's go," I told her, leaning in to kiss her once more.

"I have to take Kim home first," she replied me.

"You can't drive her like this. I'll drop her home."

"I'm not leaving my car here," she frowned.

I sighed. "I'll leave my car and I can drive yours," I offered.

"You're not driving my car," she snorted.

I pulled her closer, rubbing my hand up and down her back. I wanted to go. This was frustrating. I'm not used to girls worrying about their cars. They either didn't have one or not one nice enough to worry about. Crystal definitely had more to drink than I was comfortable with. No way was I letting her drive.

"I want to take you home," I groaned into her ear.

"I know," she whimpered back. "We can wait. I won't drink anymore."

"I have you word on that? 'Cause you're coming home with me," I said not giving her time to answer, before kissing her passionately.

"Yes, I'm coming home with you," she panted.

I could almost inhale the vibes coming off of her. This woman was no joke. I knew with everything I am, one night with Crystal was about to ruin me for life.

I wanted to leave then, but I would wait. She needed to sober up. I just hoped the time it would take her to do so wouldn't give her time to change her mind.

We danced a little more, before returning to KG's table. When we got there the waitress brought over refills of the drinks we had earlier. I pulled out a hundred and asked for some bottled water. I had a feeling KG had ordered another round but we weren't taking. I wanted Crystal to be ready to go as soon as possible.

"I like you," she whispered in my ear. "Don't play games with me, okay?"

"I want you. I'm not playing any games."

"You gonna let me take care of you, baby," she almost purred in my ear. *Damn.* I'm crazy about this woman. Did she know that?

"Yeah, Crystal, I'mma let you take care of me," I replied, cupping the back of her head to draw her into a kiss.

After a few seconds she pulled away, putting her finger to my lips. She was shaking her head at me. My brow lifted at the sudden rejection. She couldn't be changing her mind already. She smiled as laugh bubble up from her lips. She nodded her head toward KG.

"He has a big mouth. My father is picky about who I date, when I date," she winked at me. "Relax, don't worry, Daddy. I didn't change my mind."

I bit my lip. I wanted to kiss her so badly. Just the way she talked to me had me ready to explode. She always had this way of making me feel like a man around her. Crystal wasn't for boys. She made me want to man up and do right by her.

Time dragged by as we sat, whispering in each other's ear. I kept watching to see if her cousin paid us any attention. Sneaking a peck in here and there. Over an hour went by, before I noticed a change in Crystal. It was the exact moment my entire night was almost destroyed.

"Hey, Lee, is that you?" A voice called from behind me.

I turned to see Sean with his arm around Rachael's shoulder. I had forgotten all about Sean. However, it was Rachael trying to get my attention. I clenched my jaw praying she didn't say or do anything that would ruin the course the night was on—let alone any chance I had with Crystal.

"What's up, Rachael?" I said blandly.

"Nothing, just talking to your boy, Sean here," she chimed.

"I'm ready, baby," Crystal whispered in my ear.

I turned to look at her and smiled. So was I. I wanted away from Rachael and Sean. I was pissed he even brought Rachael over to this table. I couldn't for the life of me understand what the fuck he was thinking.

"Hey, Crystal," Sean crooned.

"Hey, Sean, nice to see you again," Crystal waved, but the greeting don't match her eyes. She turned back to me, lowering her voice. "Did you know he asked Brantley to get my number for him? He's a creep."

She whispered the words in my ear, sending my blood boiling. I had a bad taste in my mouth. I turned to Sean and frowned. Things were starting to become very clear.

I wrapped my arm around Crystal, ignoring her earlier concern. I took her lips in a possessive kiss that showed I was staking my claim. She smiled when I pulled away, her lips swollen from my kiss and her eyes sparkling.

Crystal shifted to get Kim's attention. She whispered something in Kim's ear. When Kim looked over Crystal's shoulder a smile greeted me this time. She whispered something back to Crystal, the exchange continuing for a few minutes.

I don't miss Kim's eyes flickering in Rachael's direction. A nasty frown coming across her face when she caught sight of her. Kim knew more about Rachael than she was saying—I was sure of that much. I wanted nothing more to do with Rachael. I had the one I wanted and she was about to leave with me.

"Let's go. Kim is leaving with KG," Crystal whispered. "She's going to distract him so we can leave."

I stood up, waiting to ensure she was steady when she walked slightly ahead of me. If she wasn't we were going to prolong the exit a little more. She moved with ease, much to my relief.

I took note of the way Sean's gaze lingered on Crystal. I tightened my fists at my side. All along he'd been bad mouthing her just so he could try to get with her.

"You out son?" Sean called.

"Yeah. I'll leave the bird watching to you," I snorted, grabbing Crystal's waist as we walked out.

When we got outside the club, we both handed the valet our tickets for our cars. Crystal was definitely sober. I could tell by the way she looked up at me seductively. The part of her that she didn't trust with me had come out to play. Her mind was made up.

Her car was the first to arrive. I walked her to her door, placing one last kiss on those delicious lips before she got into the driver's seat. Once she was safely in the car, I closed the door and tapped on the window.

"When we get to my place, you can park in the garage. I have two spots," I informed her.

"Okay, baby, see you there," she giggled and revved her engine.

I stood up to back away from the car. She took off as soon as I cleared her door. Impatient wasn't the word. Where the hell was my car? It took way too long for the valet to return with my ride. I jumped in as soon as he arrived, taking off after Crystal.

CHAPTER TEN

Turned Out

I didn't catch up to her until I got to my building. I found her waiting, parked at the side of the garage entryway. I rolled down my window to get her attention, waving for her to follow me in. Revving her engine just like outside the club, she trailed me into the lot the minute she saw me.

I pulled into my spot, pointing out my spare space for her to take. She pulled in, popping out of her car. I walked over to her and she locked her arms around my back. Our lips collided the moment we were in reach of each other. I wrapped my arms around her, taking over the kiss while slowly backing her toward the elevator.

"What took you so long?" she murmured. "I thought you changed your mind."

"They took forever with my car," I chuckled. "I didn't change a damn thing."

I cupped her face to show exactly where my head was at. It would take a lot more to keep me from seeing this night through. There could have been a flood, fire, and hurricane involved and I was still going to make it to her.

I broke the kiss when the elevator chimed at our floor. Her eyes were filled with so much lust, I thought I'd bust through my pants to satisfy the flames staring back at me.

"Good, because I've wanted you since the first time I saw you," she said as I led her off the elevator. "I bet you didn't know that."

A mischievous smile covered her lips with her revelation. I was stunned, not for the first time that evening. She was right, I had no idea.

"So why are you just saying something?"

"Baby, this isn't for everyone," she said, placing my hands on her lush ass. "I had to make sure you were worth it."

I removed one hand to unlock the door, while I gripped a hold of her full curves with the other. I bent to kiss her neck, pulling a moan from her lips. Pushing our way into the apartment, I shut the door behind us.

"So am I worth it?"

"I'm here, right?"

"Yeah," I breathed in her face, pecking her lips. "Come here, Sexy."

Her tongue darted out to wet her lips. I watched as her small hands started to unbutton my shirt. I bit my lips, reaching to lift up the hem of her dress.

From my height advantage, I could see all that ass bounce free of the fabric. Now, I've been with women that look fine as hell all dolled up, but you start to peel the layers back and find out it was all an illusion. Can I tell you that was not the case with Crystal. She lived up to all the hype in my head and then some.

Before I knew it we were in my room and I had her pinned to the wall with her legs wrapped tightly around my back. I was surprised we made it that far. I wasn't sure if we would make it to my bed. Each sweet moan she released called to a beast I didn't know was buried deep inside me.

"Lee," she whispered in my ear as my tongue took a tour of her smooth neck.

"I've got you, baby," I purred, rocking my hips into her.

I peeled the fabric of her dress from her shoulders. My brows knit when a found her breasts held up by brown patches. She giggled and mushed me in the side of the head.

"It's just tape. They peel off," she sung. "Do you have oil?"

"Like baby oil?"

"Yes, Lee," she chuckles, sliding down my front.

"Yeah, I think or coconut oil at least," I shrug.

"Get it," she winked at me, licking her lips.

She reached to squeeze me through my slacks before I turned to retrieve the oil. I'll admit I was rock hard, painfully so. I moved as fast as I could to get the oil out of my ensuite.

When I returned Crystal sat on the edge of my bed in just that tape on her breasts, that sexy thong I wanted to peel off, and heels. I couldn't wait to get my hands on all of that brown silk. Her skin was the softest I'd ever put my hands on.

I stopped before her, holding out the coconut oil I found. She took it, making sure to brush my fingers with hers. She looked up at me through her lashes.

I watched as she poured some of the oil into her palm. I took the bottle, not taking my eyes off of her. I groaned when she rubbed her palms together, then kneaded her oil slick hands over her breasts. Crystal had more than enough to fill my palms. Reaching for a single corner of the tape on her right breast to test to see if it would come loose. It peeled away with ease.

"Peel it off for me, baby," she purred.

Leaning over her, I began to peel the tape away with my teeth, slipping my tongue out to tease her nipple as soon as it popped free. Her hand cupped the back of my head, holding me to her perfect mound.

I moved to the other side to free the other breast as well. I sucked her tightened chocolate bud into my mouth, giving a hard pull. Her cries of pleasure egged me on.

I started to climb onto the bed, but she had other plans. Crystal gave me a gentle shove, causing me to step back. Her hands went to my belt, freeing it. She was serving me that sexy look through her lashes again. I didn't realize I still had a tight grip on the oil until she pried it from my fingertips once she pushed my pants down my legs.

My dick bobbed in her face, leaking with a demand for attention. I was so swollen, I throbbed with the need to find even a hint of relief. Little did I know, my girl would not disappoint.

Crystal squeezed more oil in her palms. This time she reached for my length, wrapping me in her slippery palms. I cupped the back of her head gently as her lips wrapped around my tip.

"Oh shit, girl," I groaned as she used the wetness of her mouth and the oil to ease me to the back of her throat.

My mouth dropped open in awe. She pumped and sucked like it was her birthright. Crystal had no shame in giving it her all. She got all the way into sucking me off.

Her hands twisted, her mouth worked. When she pulled back to spit on it, I was ready to propose. I mean, she spit on it and licked it clean to do it all over again. I could feel my spine tingling. I wasn't trying to go out like a punk.

I pulled back, dipping down to grasp her legs and tossed them over my shoulders. I tore her panties right from her body. My mouth watered at the sight of her wet pussy. She was soaked just from giving me head.

"Damn, baby. All of this is for me?" I looked up her body into those eyes.

"If you can handle it," she grinned back at me.

"I love a challenge," I murmured.

Dipping my head, all talking creased. I devoured her cute little petals. Her pussy tasted as good as it looked, if not better. I almost felt bad for the beating I planned to put on her, almost.

"Oh, yes, God, yes," Crystal hollered. "Lee, you wanted this shit. You better eat like it's yours."

I pushed my face further in and pressed her legs into her chest. I sucked her soul out from between her legs. I ate up all that honey, not leaving a single drop.

When she shifted above me, it drew my attention. I looked up to find her legs locked behind her head. I blinked a few times to make sure I wasn't seeing things. Sure enough, she was spread before me like a human pretzel.

Oh, yeah, I was about to make that pussy mine in every way imaginable. I moved to my nightstand swiftly to get a rubber. I peeled the packet open on my way back over to her. Once suited up, I pulled a knee on the bed. I leaned over her, lining up with her entrance. Looking up, I could see her eyes were on my dick.

I watched her watch me as I sank into her. With slow motions I gave her a few inches at a time. The sexy look on her face as she took me was one I had to commit to memory. Crystal's sex faces were enough to make me want to come.

"Damn, yes," she whimpered.

I grasped the sheets and started to dig into her juicy warmth. She was so tight and growing more mist by the second. You could hear the slapping of my pelvis to her fat ass. Her pussy even smelled so damn good as I drilled into it.

"You feel mad good. This was more than worth the wait," I said through clinched teeth.

"You feel so good. Damn, Lee, you're in my back," she cried out.

"I ain't even get started," I growled.

I pulled out and went back in for another taste. I pushed two fingers into her tightness, tapping at her spot. I licked at her ass and thighs, not missing an inch. When I felt her squeezing around my fingers, I sucked on her clit enough to set off her orgasm. When I felt it begin to hit, I shifted to sink back inside her.

I covered her mouth as her screams filled the room. I rode right through the multiples I just set off. My eyes rolling into the back of my head.

I wasn't going to last much longer with her in this position and her tight walls milking me. I moved my mouth to her bouncing mounds, pulling a tightened bud in between my lips. The keening sound it elicited was my final straw. I spilled right into the condom, roaring as I came.

I helped her to unfold her legs, massaging them as they fell to my sides. Our chests heaved against each other. I tried not to place my weight on her while easing her further up the mattress. Crashing to my side, once we're were both settled on the bed.

"You know I'm not done with you yet?" She giggled beside me when I closed my eyes.

I grin spread across my face, my lids still shut.

"I was trying to give you a break," I replied.

"Whatever," she snorted. "I got this, Daddy. You going to remember my name for the rest of your life."

I opened my eyes and turned toward her. The little evil smile on her lips turned me on. I was ready and I hadn't fully gone down in the first place.

"Careful what you ask for," we said in unison and burst into laughter.

CHAPTER ELEVEN

Morning After

Crystal was definitely without a doubt the one. She turned me out. I would've done anything she wanted. I'd never been with a woman that made me feel the way she did. I would never have thought Crystal would or could do half of what she did. She could teach a few professionals a trick or two.

I mean, damn. Her tongue game was the truth. I'm no slouch when it comes to eating pussy, but Crystal had me thinking about my life. I needed to step some shit up if I was going to be challenging her in the bedroom.

She wasn't for the weak or the lazy. I put in work that night, well into the morning. Work in the morning wasn't even a thought. I wasn't trying to come up for air or let her up either. Not that she wanted to be let up. Crystal was the truth, she matched me where I needed and challenged just the same.

I woke up the next morning with a huge grin on my face. I could smell the breakfast cooking in the kitchen. Best of all, my sheets smelled like her perfume and her sweet essence.

I got up to brush my teeth and relieve myself before I went to find her. When I got to the kitchen I came to a halt. My mouth dropped open before a huge smile took over my face.

I found her with nothing but an apron on, placing my breakfast on the table. Now that was how a man wanted to wake up. I grabbed her by the waist, pulling her into a deep kiss. She laughed into my mouth and wrapped her arms around my back.

"Good morning, Lee," she beamed.

"Good morning, sweetheart."

"Do you have practice?" She asked as I sat.

"No, films. I want to spend some time with you later."

"Oh, boo, I can't," she groaned. "I wanted to tell you yesterday but you were being a jerk. I'm closing on my first salon today, after class."

"For real!" I tried to say through a mouth full of food. I swallowed so I could talk. "Crystal, that's great!"

"I know. I'm excited! My contractor starts on Monday."

"So can we celebrate tonight?"

"My family's kind of already planning something. I'll be home until Monday."

The cute face she made at me told me she was apologetic about not having time for me. While disappointed, I was extremely happy for her. Crystal was about making things happen. I loved that about her.

"That's cool. I need to get focused for Sunday. Can I ask you something?"

"Sure."

"First, come here," I said, while reaching for her waist to bring her onto my lap. I kissed her lips as soon as she was snuggled against me. "Where is home?"

"Oh, my family lives in Westchester."

"And you don't think your father would like me?" I asked.

"I never said that," she frowned at me. "I just didn't want KG telling my business. *I* want to tell my father who I'm seeing."

"Okay, I'm just checking."

"I'll call you tonight. I just need to get going. I need to change for class and my meeting. I don't think that dress will do for either," she laughed.

"I don't want you wearing that dress anywhere," I murmured. "Take one of my sweatshirts to put over it."

She wrinkled her nose at me and I pecked her on the cheek. I wasn't backing down on this. If I'd been around before she entered that club she would have never made it inside.

"You're serious." She gasped with an eyebrow raised. "Oh wow, you're the jealous type?"

"No, but that dress is enough to make me follow you home," I teased. "Just do it for me."

"Okay," she said softly, reaching for my face to kiss me.

Much too soon, she got up and rushed off to my room to get dressed. I finished the food on my plate, getting up for seconds. As I sat eating the second helping, she came back up the hall with one of my team hoodies over her dress. She ran over to kiss me quickly, before racing for the door.

"Later," she called over her shoulder.

"Later," I called after her.

She left me with a smile plastered across my face for the rest of the day. I knew in the pit of my stomach I wasn't trying to let her go. I should have followed my instincts from jump.

Crystal was a good girl.

CHAPTER TWELVE

Perfect for Me

The best part of my weekend was the win I pulled off by the skin of my teeth. They were trying to kill me on that field. I had two hundred and fifty passing yards, one hundred and ten yards rushing, and two touchdowns. When I wasn't focused on game time, I was sulking. I missed Crystal. Everything went well at her closing but she was crazy busy trying to get everything ordered for the contractor.

I loved her ambition. She was determined to have the salon finished and running by graduation. I was sure she could do it. I never doubted her for a minute.

Tuesday's class couldn't come fast enough. Crystal promised to come stay the night with me. I would drop her off for class in the morning before practice. I'd get her there way before time.

I was elated when she walked into class with her designer overnight bag. However, when she took the seat next to me, she looked stressed. Her eyes were glued to her phone. Without releasing her gaze on the device, she leaned over and kissed me.

"Hey, baby," she murmured.

"What's wrong?"

"I can't believe this. Closing went so well and now the floors I ordered are discontinued and they don't have enough in stock to cover the whole shop. My sinks are on backorder, the stations are on backorder and my chairs. Guess what? They're on back order."

"Baby, calm down Everything is going to be fine."

"Mm, I just want to go to your place and let you hold me. Today has been so long," she pouted.

I leaned to whisper in her ear. "Daddy will make it all better."

She bit her lip, smiling at me while she put the phone away. She looked around the room to see who was watching, before motioning with her index finger for me to come to her. She grabbed the collar of my shirt and kissed me with one of these deep sexy kisses I couldn't get enough of.

"I missed you," she whispered. "Sorry, I'm so busy talking about me. How are you feeling? My dad couldn't stop talking about how hard you played this weekend?"

"I'm good," I beamed, "So you told your father about me?"

"Not really." She rushed to explain, when I frowned at her. "My dad has been following you since before we got together. My little brother said my dad likes you. I asked Ricky about you and he said my dad thinks you have a great career ahead of you if you can stay out of trouble. My father may consider me trouble for you."

"I don't understand. How are you trouble for me?" I grumbled.

"Remember, I told you my father thinks I don't stick to anything?" she asked and waited for me to nod. "That includes relationships. I've dated a few guys my father thought I should've married."

"Okay and how does that make you trouble for me?"

"He wouldn't want me getting in your head and then leaving," she explained. "You read, Lee. You already know the *Rules to Staying Focused*."

I started to ask her more questions, but class was called into session. I was curious as to how she knew so much about that book. I only mentioned reading, *Rules to Staying Focused,* to her once. The title would not explain what was in the book. I wanted to meet her father, especially if he was up on those types of books.

Class went by quickly, but we never got back to our discussion about her father. Some part of me felt she wanted it that way. Which nagged at the back of my mind.

I forgot about all of that once we were on the way to my place. My chef left dinner for two tonight. I had other plans in mind for Crystal that didn't involve her in the kitchen.

Later that night while she slept in my arms, I lay there thinking about how I'd gotten everything I wanted. I was in love with the woman I was holding. I knew when the time was right I was going to marry her without question. I didn't even need to think about that.

Hearing her talk about her salon, coupled with spending so much time at Kenny and Kim's place caused me to have thoughts of a shop of my own. I was sure that would be my first business. I just wanted to get a few things in order first. After that my next step would be finding a place to make it all happen.

To top it all off, I was on top of my game. Endorsements were flying in left and right. Now that I knew Crystal was someone I could trust, I wanted to talk to her about all of that. I knew she would have helpful ideas and advice for me.

I was absolutely getting everything I wanted. It was all lining up perfectly. With that thought, I kissed the top of her head and drifted off to sleep.

I woke up to Crystal in just her apron making my breakfast once again. I could certainly get used to that. She showered and got ready while I ate. When I finished I found her in the bedroom sitting on the bed rubbing coconut oil into her beautiful skin. A smile grew on my face as the memory of our first night surfaced in my head.

"Need some help?" I asked as I entered the room.

"I think you helped me enough last night," she replied with a small laugh. "Go get ready for practice."

"Can I pick you up after class tonight?"

"I need to study tonight. I know I won't do that here," she whined.

"What about tomorrow night? I have a meeting but I'll be free after six."

"Um, oh no, dinner with my dad."

"Baby, your schedule is as crazy as mine," I complained. "What about Friday? I have a free day on Friday."

"Friday I need to go up to the salon in the morning to handle some things. I'm sorry I want to see you too."

"So let me take you. We can spend the day together. I want to see the salon."

"Okay. We can do that for sure. Can you pick me up at six?" she beamed.

"Yeah."

"Good, now go get dressed."

I laughed as I walked away to get ready for my day. I was in such a good mood. Yes, I was a little disappointed I wouldn't get to spend time with Crystal again until Friday, but I was still happy with the knowledge she was mine.

I dropped her on campus before making my way to practice. When I got there, there wasn't one person that didn't have a comment about the smile on my face. Sean even had the nerve to have something to say. He knew where the smile came from. I'm sure he wanted to be the one smiling.

My good mood carried over into my focus during practice. I noticed that I'd even picked up some speed on the field. My arm felt great too. The coaches recognized the changes and commented on the improvements. I had a great day.

After practice I decided to go see my mother in Connecticut. I wanted to talk to her in person about Crystal. In person, she wouldn't be able to hide her true feelings. With my mom, everything shows on her face.

When I got to her house, my mother was on the phone with one of my aunts. I raided the refrigerator for something to eat, before making myself comfortable on the couch in front of the TV. I made myself right at home.

I always loved going to see my mom. She would spoil me with attention. As a matter of fact, it didn't take her long to hang up on my aunt to focus on me.

"Hey honey, what brings you this way?" my mom asked.

"What, I can't just come see my mom?"

"No," she laughed. "Now, what you want?"

"I want to talk."

"About?" she asked as she sat next to me, reaching to rub my head.

"Crystal," I smiled. "My girlfriend. Ma she's the real deal."

"I was just waiting to see how long it was going to take you to tell me."

I frowned at my mother's words. *Kim*, I should have known. My mother and Kim always seem to have the scoop on my life before I do. I swear they have little meetings about what I'm up to or getting into.

"Aw man, Kim can't hold water." I huff. I couldn't even be mad. I just had to laugh. "So what do you know?"

"I know she's a beautiful young lady and she's in love with you. I know you almost messed up big time. I thought I taught you better than to have girls crying over you," she replied, slapping the back of my head.

"I ain't have nobody crying," I pouted like I was still ten.

"That's not how Kim told it. This Crystal likes you more than you think. What you did that day hurt her feelings, Lee. Boy, I know I taught you better than that."

"I didn't know that, Ma. I wouldn't hurt Crystal on purpose. I'm in love with her," I spoke my thoughts out loud.

"She sounds like a great girl. Kim spoke very highly of her. We both know Kim doesn't like anyone, especially when it comes to her Lee."

My mom laughed at her own words. Kim being the oldest had always been over protective of Kenny and me. She looked out for me from the time we were little.

"Yeah, Crystal is great. She's smart, beautiful, ambitious, and she can cook. Boy, can that girl cook. And she knows how to treat me. She makes me feel like a man and makes me want to be a better one."

"So when do I get to meet her?"

I shrugged. "I don't know, right now, I'm trying to get time with her. Our schedules are crazy and she's always so busy."

"Well, when you two have time, I would like to meet her. Even if I have to come to New York."

"Yes, ma'am."

I hung out with my mom for a while before heading back home. Crystal called while I was there, causing my mother to tease me relentlessly. Apparently, I had a huge grin on my face during the call. My mom went in on me for cheesing so hard. I love that my mother and I have that type of relationship.

On my way home, I thought about what my mother said about Crystal and her feelings for me. It bothered me that I made Crystal cry that day at the shop. I was a jerk.

I had a lot to make up for. I should have handled all of that a lot better. It showed immaturity on my part. I needed to start thinking out my actions, especially if I wanted to hold onto a woman like Crystal.

My mind started to think about our future. The campus wasn't that far from my place and I had the extra parking spot. Crystal could move in with me and we could spend way more time together. It would solve one of our biggest issues.

I would let her study. I knew how important that was to her. I also wanted her to go to my next away game. I knew how busy she was, but I would love for her to make it.

I had a lot to think about and some planning to do. I was going to tell Crystal how I felt about her and soon. I'd always been a man about his. It was how I got as far as I had in the league. I went after the challenges before me until I won the prize. I knew my desired end results. It was time to bring it all to fruition.

Crystal was what I'd always hoped for and I wasn't trying to let that slip away. According to her plan, things were lining up nicely. We both fit together and into the vision we had for the future. This was the life, the dream.

Everything about Crystal was flawless and perfect for me. I couldn't have picked a better woman. What could go wrong?

CHAPTER THIRTEEN

Her Business

Friday rolled around and I greeted the day at four in the morning. I missed Crystal so much I couldn't sleep. Restless, I got out of bed, cleaned up, put fresh sheets on the bed, and changed the towels in the bathroom.

I quickly made something to eat, before running through some emails and studying some new plays. When five fifteen rolled around I almost ran out of the door. I arrived at the dorm a little before six, but Crystal was already downstairs.

I opened the trunk for her things, getting out to toss them inside for her. When I moved to open her door, I almost attacked her. Cupping her face in my hands, I kissed her like it was the last time I would ever get the chance.

Crystal clung to my jacket, lifting on her toes to get closer. Her breathing came out in pants when I broke the seal on our lips. I was greeted with a giggle as she pressed her forehead to my chest. I leaned down to kiss the back of her hair, my arms going around her back to hold her tightly to me.

"I missed you too," she breathed.

"Sorry. Good morning," I chuckled back. "You look great."

"Good morning, honey. Thank you," she lifted her head to beam up at me. "Did you eat?"

"Yeah."

"Okay. I'll program your GPS for the salon."

"Alright."

I released her to allow her to get into the car once I opened the door. As soon as she was settled, I jogged around to the driver's side to climb in. I leaned to peck her lips before putting my seatbelt on. She punched in the address while I stroked her cheek with my fingertips.

"Okay, all set. Let's go. Craig got on my nerves all day yesterday. They're getting things done faster than I can get the materials. I need to make sure the right sinks and stuff were delivered before they can put them in."

From the focused look in her eyes and the firmness of her tone, I knew she was all business. It was sexy. The drive and determination tuned me on.

"Alright, I'll get you there don't worry," I replied as my chest swelled.

My girl was about her business. I would do my part to get her there so she could take care of things. I couldn't wait to see her in her element.

I thought we'd get to talk on the way, but Crystal was on the phone with her contractor as soon as we pulled off. They were arguing from the beginning. I listened to her hold her ground though. I found that very attractive. I will admit though, a part of me wanted to step in as her man. Yet, I could also see she could handle herself.

When we got to the address the GPS led me to, Crystal pointed out a parking lot for me to turn into. I maneuvered into the lot she signaled me toward and parked. It was an impressive looking area.

"Listen, Craig, I'm here. I'll be inside in a minute," she said into the phone and hung up. "Do you like my parking lot?" she turned to me and chimed.

"This is yours?" I asked looking around at the huge lot we were in.

"Yup, I had to have it. I want my customers to have a place to park and not have to worry about finding a spot or feeding meters."

"You're amazing, you know that?" I said, leaning to kiss her.

"Mm-um, business first baby."

I smiled at her, turning to get out and open her door. I reached for her hand as we walked out of the lot. We turned to the right of the lot and I could see the men moving in and out of her salon. From the outside the place looked huge.

When we stepped inside the floors were covered with brown paper and blue painters tape. Crystal released my hand to bend down and peel back a section of the paper. I could see the mahogany hardwood flooring with glass and silver tile inlays that were hidden underneath the covering. I watched the smile that spread across her face as the floors come into view.

While she inspected the floors, a light skinned tall brother made his way towards us with a tight expression on his face. He scowled down at Crystal as he got closer. Crystal stood up, closing the distance between them.

I reached for her hand again to let him know we were together. I didn't like the look on his face. I wanted to make it clear she wasn't alone.

"Craig, this is Lee, Lee, this is Craig, my contractor." Crystal made quick introductions.

"Nice to meet you," Craig grumbled as I nodded at him, he turned to start ranting at Crystal. "Crystal I need…wait Lee Johnson?"

Craig stopped, cutting off in the middle of his sentence to turn back towards me. Recognition lit his eyes and his mouth dropped open. It was still a reaction I hadn't gotten used to from fans.

"Yes," I replied.

He stuck out his hand and I returned the gesture, shaking his hand. He's entire demeanor changed.

"Oh man, my son loves you. You've been doing great, man. Keep up the great work," he crooned. "Can I have your autograph? It would mean so much to my kid."

"No problem," I answered.

"Wait just a minute. Let me get a piece of paper and a pen or something."

Crystal had already walked off toward a stack of boxes. She had a boxcutter out, slicing them open to peel back the tops and peek inside them. I walked up behind her and placed my hands on her waist. Her face turned up to look at me. The smile on her face was adorable as she beamed.

"You want to see my sinks?" she cooed.

"Of course."

"I had to have these. They're glass basins with paint set inside the glass. Aren't they beautiful?"

I looked in the box, revealing the clear sinks with silver paint embedded inside the glass. They were luxurious and sophisticated. Much like the owner of the shop.

She moved to some other boxes, waving me over.

"These are the stations, similar concept. I wanted to go with a glamorous modern feel," she explained.

I looked into the box to see one of the stations. It was clear with silver streaks of paint in between the glass panels. One side had a silver panel that kept it from being completely see-through.

"This all looks great," I said as I pulled her into a hug her. "I'm excited for you."

"So are we good, Crystal? Can my guys start?" Craig asked as he returned with paper and a marker.

"So far so good," she chimed.

I took the paper and marker from him. "What's your son's name?" I noticed that Craig had even changed his tone towards Crystal.

"Tyrell. Guys, let's get these sinks and stations going," he called over his shoulder.

"Craig, you take care of my baby's place and I'll make sure you and your son get to enjoy a few games at the stadium. That sound fair?"

"Lee," Crystal sighed, reaching to pinch me.

"What?"

She only gave me a shy smile. I winked at her, reaching for her to come closer. Tucking her into my side, I dipped to kiss the top of her head.

"That sounds fair. My guys do great work. We're just having trouble working around Crystal's schedule," Craig huffed.

"Get in line," I laughed.

"Do you want to see the rest of the place?" Crystal snorted.

"Sure."

"His guys truly are fast. They already finished the rental properties."

"Rentals? This place is huge."

"Yeah, that's why I had to have it. There are rental units upstairs. I'll take you up when we're finished with the tour down here."

As we walked to the back of the salon, I could get a better sense of how large the place actually was. It had a nice open feel. Yet, it was all inviting. Crystal's face lit up as we walked through.

"Here's where the sinks will be," she said while pointing out a wall in the back of the shop. "Over here, in this room will be the brow and lash area. These two rooms next to it are the massage rooms." She pulled me to the other side. "Over here will be the body waxing rooms."

She kept a firm hold of my hand as she dragged me back toward the front of the place. Craig followed us as he barked orders to his staff. I could see that a few of his guys wanted to ask for an autograph as well. However, from the look on Craig's face I'm sure he wasn't having it.

"Here's where the stylists will be set up on each side and my station will be here in the center. Craig is putting in glass waterfalls for partitions, which will separate the fellas from the ladies. The front of the place will be all barbers. In the very front where the boxes are will be the waiting area and the reception desk."

Crystal glowed as she filled me in. I could imagine everything she explained. The place was going to be phenomenal

"This looks like it's going to be great."

I was so proud of her. Her dream was coming true right before our eyes. I wanted that for her.

"Come on, I want to show you upstairs."

Again she pulled me along, looking just like an excited schoolgirl. Her head bounced back and forth, taking in my reaction and looking things over for herself. The smile on her face was priceless.

We went outside and entered a door to the far right of the salon. Crystal walked up a flight of stairs as I followed. We entered a long hallway with four doors. Men were in and out of the door on the right, furthest from us. Crystal went to the first unit, opening the door.

"There are four units, all two bedrooms. I had new hardwoods put in, all new fixtures and stainless steel appliances. Granite countertops in the kitchens and bathrooms."

We walked through each room as she showed the place off. The apartment was off the hook. She had them paint it neutral colors and the open floor plan was spot on. Crystal was unquestionably about her business.

"I'm going to list them next week. What do you think?" she asked looking concerned.

"Baby, this is poppin'. You're doing a great job, Ma. For real."

"Thanks," she sighed.

We returned to the salon. From the moment we entered, Crystal and Craig were at it again. Although, I could tell he was more cautious now that I was there. I took a step back and let my girl handle her business.

Craig was only making things harder on himself. Crystal was going to get what she wanted anyway. Everything he challenged her on, he turned around and agreed to. It was actually comical.

"Sorry, baby, Craig is good at what he does, but he can be bullheaded," Crystal said as she came over to me, locking her arms around my waist.

"It's okay. You take care of your business."

"Give me a few more minutes to see what Craig is talking about and we can go."

"No problem. Take your time."

"You're the best, come here for a minute," she said reaching for my face.

I bent into her kiss while she lifted up on her toes. Everyone around us disappeared. Anything other than the woman before me was forgotten. They were still moving in and out of the salon, but our focus remained on each other as I deepened the kiss.

My hands moved to her hips, drawing her to me. I had a tight hold of her while devouring her lips. We were lost in each other when I heard someone come through the front door, clearing their throat. Crystal pulled away quickly to look toward the door.

"Oh, hey, Daddy," she chimed. "Um, Daddy, I want you to meet Lee Johnson. Lee, this is my father, Gregory Livingston."

I turned to look to the man who had just entered the building. It took a few seconds for reality to set in. I was in total shock. Crystal's father was Greg Livingston. *The* Greg Livingston. I never thought about her last name. I know so much about Mr. Livingston. I scanned my brain. He never mentioned a daughter named Crystal.

He and his wife have four kids. The oldest son Gregory Jr., there next oldest was Henry, a daughter, Coco, and their youngest son, Richard. Crystal called her younger brother Ricky. That's when it clicked. KG kept calling her Coco. I never realized when Greg Livingston talked about his daughter he was using a nickname. That was why it was ringing in my head the other night, but I couldn't place it.

Now I understood why Kenny and Kim thought I was being so stupid and why the whole thing was so funny to them. I totally understood what Crystal meant about the book, *Rules to Staying Focused*. Her father wrote it. How had I been so slow?

I quickly pulled myself together, sticking out my hand to shake his. This was such an honor. He looked me over before taking my hand. I wasn't sure if Crystal had been right about her father liking me. Maybe it was the fact that he just caught me trying to swallow his daughter's face.

"Nice to meet you, Sir," I said as I firmly shook his hand.

"Lee Johnson, impressive game last weekend. I've been wanting to meet you."

"Wow, Sir. I've really been wanting to meet you. I've read your books. That's what made me enter the MBA program."

He raised a brow, turning to look at Crystal.

"You've read my books? Really?" he chuckled.

Immediately my mind went back to the conversation Crystal and I last had about her father. I knew he was inferring to what Crystal implied, about her being trouble. I wasn't sure how to feel about that.

"Crystal," Craig called, pulling her attention.

She looked up at me nervously biting her lip before rushing off to see what Craig wanted.

"So Lee, if you read my books, what are your intentions with my daughter?" Mr. Livingston asked.

"Sir, Crystal is on my priority list. I have the game and school in the right perspective. Now, I have Crystal in the right place to complete my goal. Sir, I intend to make her a part of my life," I responded.

"You should stay focused, but Crystal has grown up a lot this past year. This place proves that. I hope she sticks to you with the same determination. You have a bright future," he said sternly. "If Coco is what you want, I suggest you make sure up front, you're what she wants."

"Yes, Sir."

"Daddy, what brings you here?" Crystal asked as she returned, cutting off the intense conversation.

"Your mother is looking for you. She asked me to stop by and see if I could catch you."

"Oh, no... what now?" Crystal whined. "If she isn't calling my phone, she wants something I need to run away from."

"You know your mother, honey," Mr. Livingston chuckled. "She wants you to come up to the house."

"Would it be okay if we stop at my parents' place?" she asked.

"Sure, no problem."

"Thanks. I promise it won't take long," she said, but wrinkled her nose at her father.

"Don't make promises you can't keep," he laughed.

"Daddy, we have plans. Mommy can't hold me hostage today," she pouted.

"You can't blame your parents for wanting to spend a little time with you Coco." Her father cared about her, you could see it in his eyes and the way he talked to her.

"Okay," she huffed. "Well, I just wrapped up here. Ready?"

"Yes." I answered.

"Make sure you're driving safely with my little girl," her father said and kissed her forehead.

"No problem, Sir."

My head was still reeling from the fact that Greg Livingston was Crystal's father. I mean this guy is huge in person. Crystal is a little thing. I towered over her at six-five and her dad was taller than me.

I would never have thought the way she talks about her budgets that her father was Greg Livingston. Crystal didn't need my money. Her father's money made what I have look like cheese on a mouse trap.

We all left out, heading for the parking lot. Her father climbed into his grey Bentley, while we got into my car. Once we were in the car, she entered the address to her parents' house in the GPS.

"Why didn't you tell me who your father is?" I asked.

"You of all people should understand. You're not the only one with groupies," she scoffed. "People get stupid when they know I have money."

"I guess I understand that," I mused. "But Ma, you thought I would trip."

"I don't know. I was going to tell you. I just wanted to see where this was going. If…if you feel the same way about me as I feel about you," she said softly.

I leaned over and kissed her.

"Crystal, I love you and who your father is has no effect on that either way."

I told her while rubbing my nose to hers. I let my words hang between us while they sunk in. I knew how I felt and I had already resolved that I planned to tell her.

"I love you too. Baby, I've never felt this way about anyone."

Her words caused me to beam down at her. My chest filled with joy. It was one thing for my mother to tell me Crystal had feelings for me, but another to hear it out of her mouth for myself.

"Maybe we better go. My father will worry if we are too far behind him," she said as she stared into my eyes.

I started the car, following the instructions the GPS started to call out.

CHAPTER FOURTEEN

Meet the Family

It didn't take us long to get to the large estate Crystal called home. Pulling up to the gates made me feel more embarrassed about the thoughts I once had about Crystal. She was so far from a gold digger.

I had signed a nice contract and gotten some great endorsements, but I still wasn't in a comfortable enough place to do this for her. This place screamed wealth and planning. It said those behind the doors knew what they wanted in life and made it happen.

I was still in the planning stages for all of this to come. I started to question whether I was even worth Crystal's time after all. Clearly, I needed to step things up to be with her. Her father was one of the men I looked up to as a mentor. I needed to accomplish some of my goals to even look like I'd been a worthy mentee.

Excitement covered Crystal's face as we got to the front of the house. I have to admit I had become nervous. I wondered if her mother would like me. I still wasn't that sure about her father. It seemed like he was cool with me dating Crystal.

"Park right up front," Crystal nodded in the direction she was suggesting.

I got out of the car to open her door so she could climb out. She eagerly grabbed my hand, pulling me along through the large front doors of the house. Her face lit up as she watched for my reaction to the house.

The place was beautiful. The kind of house you dreamed about. As I looked around and then back at her, it all fit together. She looked like she belonged in this house. I couldn't see how I had missed it before, but Crystal looked like money. Pictures of her coming to class all dressed up, started to flash in my head. I could see what I had been missing all along.

"What are you thinking?" she stopped to ask.

"This place is huge. I have a lot of work to do to give you what you deserve." I said the first thing that came to mind.

After I said it I wasn't so sure I meant to be that honest. I looked down at my feet, my brows drawn together. This all caught me off guard.

"See, that's why I don't tell guys who my family is. I don't want you to think you have to do what my father does. It took him time to build this," she said, reaching up to cup my face. "Time and a great woman by his side. You can have this and give it to me, but that work will not just be yours. Don't let this intimidate you."

"See, that's why I love you," I crooned, dipping to kiss her.

"I love you too," she giggled. "Let's go find my mom."

"Alright."

"Mommy," she started to call through the house. "Mom."

"I'm in the kitchen, Crystal. How many times do I have to tell you kids not to call through the house," I heard a woman's voice call back to her.

We turned a corner and entered a large kitchen area. There was a woman dressed like a maid at the sink and another woman at the bar counter sitting on a stool with a bunch of magazines, a legal pad, and what looked like checklists. I could tell right away she was Crystal's mom. They looked like twins. The woman stood up the moment she saw us.

"Hey Coco, who do we have here?" her mother sang.

"Mommy, I want you to meet Lee. Lee, this is my mother." Crystal looked so proud to introduce me to her mother, which made me feel good.

"Nice to meet you, Mrs. Livingston," I reached out to shake her mother's hand, but she stepped forward to hug me.

"Nice to meet you," she chimed. "Crystal, are we keeping secrets?"

"No, Mommy. I just wasn't sure I was ready to bring him home." She shrugged and bit her lip as she looked at me.

"So does this mean Lee will be escorting you to your ball?"

"Mommy, that's in four months."

"And you need to pick a dress and have his tux coordinated."

"He works on weekends," Crystal whined.

"Well, four months is plenty of time to give notice to get the day off."

Mr. Livingston entered the kitchen laughing at their exchange. "Honey, the NFL does not just give their starting quarterback the day off for his girlfriend's graduation party," he teased.

"Oh! You're a player. Coco how did that happen?" her mother snorted in the same cute way she does.

"Mommy," Crystal grumbled and gave her a look.

My curiosity was peaked. I wondered what exactly that was all about. I looked at Crystal, but she wouldn't look at me. When a few beats passed I decided to relieve some of the tension.

"Actually, Crystal I meant to tell you, I checked and we have a home game that weekend. I want to be your escort."

"Really?" she turned towards me this time. She threw her arms around my waist. "Thank you."

"No problem."

"Finally, so we can go dress shopping tomorrow," her mother sighed.

"I have plans with Lee this weekend." Crystal huffed.

"Well, we need to start looking Coco or you can have one made as I've been suggesting."

I liked her mother, she was funny. I see where Crystal gets her determination to get what she wants. I could see Crystal would cater to her mother's requests one way or another. It was only a matter of time.

"What's up, sis," a tall built looking kid called as he entered the kitchen.

Crystal's face lit up as he came to hug her. She held his hand while turning to look up at me. Again she looked proud to be able to introduce me to her family.

"Ricky, this is Lee."

"Oh word! What's up man? My sister has been asking me all types of questions about you."

Immediately he looked like he didn't mean to blurt that out. Crystal frowned, throwing an elbow at him. Ricky reached to rub his ribs.

"Nice to meet you," I chuckled.

"You've been doing your thing out there."

"Thanks, I told your sister you should come out to a game. I'll give her my home game dates. Just let me know when you want to come."

"I'm with it. Coco, what's good?" He crooned with excitement.

"If you want to go," she shrugged.

"Crystal, I would love if you would come this weekend. I can get you guys in the skybox."

"Is that cool with you, Ricky?" she asked.

"Yeah, Coco, *please*."

"Okay," she giggled.

"Mr. Livingston, I would be honored if you would come too."

I wasn't trying to suck up. I actually wanted him to come to my game. I mean, he knows the game, the league, everything.

"A chance to spend time with my Coco, I don't see why not," Mr. Livingston replied.

"Well, speaking of time. Mommy, Lee and I have plans tonight. I know you wanted something. What's up?" Crystal went over to her mother and rested her arms on her shoulders.

"I had a great idea. Since the salon will be finished by the party, I thought we should promote the grand opening. I found some great ideas," her mother sang, pointing to some things she found in her magazines.

Crystal switched into business mode again. Her father winked at me and laughed. He nodded for me to follow him out of the kitchen. I figured we weren't leaving anytime soon. I didn't mind. I always wanted a chance to sit in a room with Mr. Livingston to pick his brain.

Pick his brain is exactly what I did. He quizzed me for about two hours and then he let me have my turn. We talked about the game, how to stay on top of my finances, watching my agent, being aware of decisions and changes around me, and balancing it all. We talked more in detail about Crystal too.

Her father truly wants the best for her. He said she has a habit of finding guys that are ideal and walking away from them. I had my own questions about that.

I did consider that this could totally be his opinion, but I wanted to know more about the fact. There had to be more that lead him to his beliefs. I guess my questions were written all over my face.

"There's a reason I refused to pay for Coco to go to school. That girl would start something new every week. Usually right after quitting whatever it was she just started.

"Let me see. There was singing lessons, piano, did you know she was in a group with her cousin, KG," he chuckled and shook his head. "At one point, she was dancing in his videos. Then she was his stylist. There was the time she wanted to be a stewardess and fly around the world. Oh, and a race car driver. I blame her giving up on that one on her mother.

"It didn't stop there though. She's the same with relationships. Coco loses interest in things. I wanted her to learn the cost of starting something and not finishing. I know I spoil my daughter, but I think not paying her tuition was one of the best things I could ever do for her."

"She finished," I chuckled.

"That she did. She had to work for it and this time she had boundaries. Being told no made her determined to have it," his smile broadened. "I'm damn proud of that girl. She not only stuck to it. She exceled at it. Her grades have been remarkable and she did it all full-time."

"She's amazing," I said proudly.

"She sure is. I watched her map it all out and execute her plan. The girl is damn smart," he nodded.

"Yeah, she is."

His next words answered a question I'd been wondering about. Crystal is a full time student and she's paying her own way through school. If her parents aren't helping the money has to come from somewhere.

"You have no idea. Did you know she goes around and consults salons on how to increase their revenue? She does hair in their shops every now and then to make some cash.

"In addition, she trains their stylists. Made enough the first year to pay for her tuition and the dorm. She has a gift for those salons.

The more I learned about Crystal the more into her I became. When she and her mother were done they came to the study we were in. Her mother took her turn getting to know me while telling me stories about her daughter.

As usual, Crystal was doing Crystal. She made sure I ate and had plenty to drink. Every chance she got, she placed her hands on me in small comforting gestures. Touching my knee, my face, my shoulder—every now and then—casually placing a hand on my chest.

We left her parents' house pretty late, after they insisted we stay for dinner with them. When we arrived at my place Crystal was wiped out. I had a million questions I wanted to ask her.

However seeing her exhaustion, I held them all in. I let her shower sorting my thoughts while I waited. When she came out, I massaged her back while she fell asleep.

I figured I would have plenty of time to ask all of my questions later. I wasn't going anywhere and I was almost sure that neither was she. Hopefully, I was something she would stick to.

CHAPTER FIFTEEN

Move In?

I was hyped on Sunday to play with Crystal and her family in the box, especially her dad. It showed in my game. I had five hundred yards passing, forty yards rushing, and three touchdowns.

After the game I got Crystal's father and brother access to the locker room. A few of the players talked to Ricky about the game, which got him charged up. I could see in his eyes he went from wanting to play to needing to play.

I was happy I could help. Mr. Livingston looked happy to see Ricky focused on the game, while deciding to become more dedicated. A few of the guys on the team surrounded Mr. Livingston. Each one trying to get information and pointers. It made me feel privileged that I'd gotten a one on one with him.

After the game, Mr. Livingston took us all out to dinner. I could see how excited Crystal had been for me. She mentioned it was the first time she'd gotten a chance to see me play.

She doesn't watch sports a lot. She went to her brother's games as much as she could to support him, but she wasn't one to faithfully sit and watch. She understood the game though. It was cute to hear her talk about the numbers I put up and different plays from the game.

On the way home, she made it a point to let me know how excited she was to see me play. I needed to get home before she made me crash my car. I was holding on by a thread. I was already charged up from the win.

She leaned into me, placing a hand on my thigh. My dick twitched in my pants. Stopping at a light, I turned to look her. I could see the mischief in his eyes. Kissing those full lips quickly, I turned back toward the road.

"I'm so proud of you, Baby," she whispered in my ear.

"Crystal," I warned.

"Yes," she purred. "Tell me what you want. I want to show my man just how proud of him I am."

"I want to beat that pussy up right," I licked my lips, looking out the corners of my eyes.

"Mm, you can do that. But let me tell you what I plan to do for my man," she said, squeezing me through my pants. "I'm going to lick you from head to toe. I want to taste every single inch of you. When I'm done, I'm going to climb onto your face and ride it while I suck the cum right out of your—

"Shit," I hissed, slamming on the breaks.

Crystal tried not to laugh, but it slipped through her lips. I turned to narrow my eyes at her. I'd almost run into the back of the car in front of us.

"Focus, Mr. Johnson," she taunted.

"I got your Mr. Johnson," I muttered.

"Yes, baby. You do," she sang, reaching to cup my strained erection once more.

She sat back in her seat, bouncing her leg over her other thigh. I did everything I could not to run a light or get a speeding ticket. I was almost ready to burst. All the dirty things going through my head. I planned to work that ass out.

However, something changed though when we got to my place. Crystal went into the bathroom to get ready for bed. I sat waiting for her to come out, still turned on from the ride home.

Something shifted when she stepped into the room dressed in a pink silk nightgown. I saw her differently For the first time, I saw my wife.

My throat tightened, my mouth went dry. I could feel my heart racing. It all hit me like a ton of bricks.

I could see me married to her. This woman coming to me like this every night. I mean, I knew I would marry her, but this was the first time I *really* saw her.

This was different. I didn't want to just have sex. I wanted to make love to her. I wanted her to feel what I felt when I looked at her.

It was the first time I had ever been nervous to have sex with someone. It was crazy. We'd slept together already, but somehow this was different—new in a way. It was all about her and showing her how much she meant to me.

I reached for her waist as she stopped in front of me. My hands slid over the silky fabric around to her plump ass. I palmed her globes, pulling her body into me.

Her nipples strained against the fabric insistently calling for my attention. I licked my lips, holding back. My hands traveled down to her thighs, moving back up underneath the soft fabric covering her body. Her smooth warm skin heated my palms.

I groaned when I found her bare ass greeting my palms. Moving my hands down slightly, I grasped her thighs, lifting her to drop her into my lap. She wiggled until she settled over my erection.

I took her lips in a soft, slow kiss. It didn't take long for the kiss to deepen. We came at each other from every angle. Tongue and teeth clashing, moans and groans mingling. My hands moved to cup her breasts as her hands moved to cup the back of my head.

Her hips started a slow rock against my length. Wrapping one around her waist, I moved back on the bed taking her with me. I flipped her on her back, climbing over her body. The scent of her body wash bounced up, hitting my nostrils as she hit the sheets.

I moved my face to her neck, sucking her flesh into my mouth. The sharp intake of her breath brought a smile to my lips. I was glad to only be in my boxers. The less between us the better, which led me to peeling away the gown clinging to her beautiful skin.

I let my tongue and lips do the exploring as I worked my way down her body. Her musical sighs and pleas guiding me to her pleasure. I savored the taste of her as she became my personal playground. Words could not explain the swelling in my chest.

I settled between her legs and devoured her honey. I had a deep conservation with her lower lips. Telling her how much I loved her, talking to her pussy like it was my best friend.

I was rewarded with her confirmation of her love for me with her verbal promises of love and dedication. The more she declared, the deeper I pressed in, affirming my own devotion into her folds.

"I love you," she cried. "Yes, don't stop. You know it's yours."

Hearing her words punched me through the chest. I hummed into her core, enjoying her sweetness as I devoured her. Her fingers locked on the back of my head holding me between her legs as she rode my face.

"I'm coming again," she whimpers.

My skin heated as desire filled me to the brink. Sweat poured down my face while I worked for it. Each orgasm I licked and sucked from her body a labor of love. The feel of her body trembling and quaking before me better than winning any game.

"Lee, please," she begged.

I lapped up the gift from my efforts. Pulling away I stared at her glistening lips, smacking my lips. Best meal I've ever had came from between her thick brown thighs.

I pushed my boxers down my hips climbing over her body. Reaching into the nightstand, I retrieved a condom. Thoughts of filling her belly with our children floated through my mind. I pushed that to the side for the moment, suiting up instead.

I dipped my head allowing her to taste herself on my lips. Crystal's little freaky ass licked my mouth clean, sucking on my face and lips for good measure.

I cupped her face with one hand, planting the other by her head. I was so hard, I didn't need my hand to line up with her wet entrance to slide in. I poked once, twice, sinking the third try. Her wet warm sucked my right in.

"I love you," she breathed.

"I love you too, baby," I groaned.

It's as if we completed each other. She was made for me and I for her. Flawless—that's how we fit together. She met every motion and gesture of mine with absolute completion. We were the perfect complement to one another.

Her fingernails dug into my back. Our bodies creating a language of their own. So many emotions swirled around and through us, I felt as if I could taste them.

I reached for her legs to bring them onto my shoulders. Still keeping the pace slow, I drew us closer and closer. I could feel her clenching around me, milking me for the seed I tried to hold onto for a bit longer.

When her eyes locked on mine, showing me her love, I couldn't hold back any longer. I came with a roar as she trembled beneath with her own release. I couldn't have timed it better if I tried.

I pulled out, rolling to my side. Crystal turned into my embrace when I reached to wrap her in my arms. Her small limbs wrapped around my body, clinging to me lazily. I held her basking in the fact that we just made love. It was a deeper level, a change occurred between us.

Time passed without either of us saying a word. Our breathing the only sound in the room. Neither of us moved an inch. My semi-erect penis still wearing the condom I spilled in. Crystal shifted closer, pressing her face to my chest.

"Can I ask you something?" I asked as I traced her shoulder with my fingers.

"Anything," she answered nestling her face into my chest.

"What did your mother mean the other day? When she mentioned me being a player. She asked how'd that happen?'"

"Oh, you caught that," she sighed. "I don't date athletes. At least, I try very hard not to."

"Why not?"

"Let's just say I had an interesting childhood. My father didn't help the way I see pro athletes."

"Oh, okay." From her tone, I decided to leave it at that. It seemed like it was a sort of sore subject. "Can I ask you something else?"

"Yup."

"I know you said you don't stick to relationships. Why not?"

"I always know they're not the one. I mean, I have dated some nice guys, but having set finances and a great career doesn't make a husband for me, the way it does for my father. I want more."

"What makes a husband for you?" I asked nervously.

I had a hundred thoughts running through my head at the time. I wanted her answer to be me. I wanted her to claim me as her ideal man.

"I want someone that I can look at and see that he loves me," she mused. "You know, someone that wants to protect me and keep me happy. Someone that I can look at and without a word, know I'm what he wants."

She lifted her head from my chest to look up at me. Leaning in she pecked my lips.

"So how long does it take you to know they're not it?"

"I don't know. Sometimes, I knew from the start," she shrugged. "But I still dated them to please my father, others maybe a month or two."

"Oh."

We hadn't been together more than a month technically. I still wasn't in the safe zone.

"Lee, baby?"

"Yes."

"I knew you were the one the first time I saw you," she said softly and touched my face. "You walked in our first class together, looking so confident and focused. I wanted to talk to you, but I couldn't allow myself to be distracted. I noticed how you would watch me and some part of me wanted you to talk to me. But another part wanted nothing to do with you because I knew I wouldn't walk away from you. I wanted you.

"That's why I tried to change research partners in the beginning. I knew spending anytime with you would've led me here. The night I first kissed you, I made Nichelle promise to make sure I went home. I would've stayed if you asked me too. I would've made her break her promise.

"I fought with what I wanted that night I made you dinner and you kissed me. I had almost changed my mind to take things forth, but when you got that phone call you looked like you wanted to go. I figured you didn't want me to stay as much as I wanted to.

"From there, I knew it was only a matter of time. I was already falling for you. I didn't understand you that day at Kim and Kenny's. I was so hurt. I thought I did something wrong, but that night in the club I just wanted you. I don't know... it's hard to explain I just don't know how to not want you."

"Crystal about that, I'm sorry about the way I acted. I didn't mean to hurt you. I would never do that on purpose. I was an asshole. A stupid asshole."

Before I could go any further, she put her finger to my lips, lifting herself to get face to face with me. She sat silent for a second, staring in my eyes. Her orbs searching my face as her finger traced the line of my jaw. I moved to kiss her, but she shook her head.

"I forgive you for that. I understand this is all new to you. You want to be sure you're making the right decisions. I just want you to know you can trust me. I'm not looking for anything from you but a chance to love you and to be loved by you. I know how to make my own, if anything, baby. I want to make you better, help you get to where you want to be."

"I want you to move in with me," I blurted out without thinking.

It was my truth. I'd been thinking about it for days. It was a step in the direction I needed us to go.

"Are you serious?" she asked searchingly.

"Yeah, I mean it. I want you to live with me. I love you."

"Lee, I don't know. Are you sure?"

"Is it that you don't know because you're not sure about me or because you don't think it's a good idea?"

"Have you been listening?" she giggled. "I love you and I'm positive about you. It's just…that's big. Are you sure you want me in your space?"

"Yes, Crystal. I want you in my space. I want more than that but this is a step there."

"Can I think about it?"

"Yeah," I answered, not hiding my disappointment well.

"Okay, I thought about it. When do I move in?" she giggled.

"Tomorrow, please. I'll take you to get your things. If you want you can get your car from the lot and use my other space."

"You do know I take up a lot of closet space?" she teased.

"I don't care, as long as you're here."

"I love you, Lee. I want to make you happy."

"You do, Baby. You make me very happy."

CHAPTER SIXTEEN

It all falls Down

Crystal had everything moved out of her dorm room by the following weekend after I asked her to move in. I knew she had a financial plan that living with me and commuting didn't include. So I paid for her parking and gas expenses despite our dispute over it at first.

Living together worked out great. Crystal had me focused on everything. She took great care of me. She packed my things for my away games. She would help me relax the night before home games. Giving me massages and cooking me dinner. She was there to support and comfort me for the few losses I did have.

I supported her and the salon as well. I went with her to check on the place as much as I could. She and Craig still argued, but I think that was just a Craig and Crystal thing. It all paid off in the end.

The place came out amazing. Crystal's vision truly came to life. I was so damn proud of her.

I wanted to support my baby as much as I could. I started telling some of the players I trusted to have their wives and girlfriends go to support my girl.

Time was moving fast. We had finished our project early and coasted through the rest of the class. Our professor was more than impressed by our work and we received the A we both worked so hard for. Crystal of course aced all of her final classes. Moving in with me didn't cause her to lose focus one bit.

Crystal educated me on a lot. I mean I'm no dummy, but I never had anyone to take the time to show me the real deal with financial planning. I had played it by ear and moved from what I read for myself before I met her. She taught me to live, not spend or be scared to circulate.

We had gone house hunting a few times. We knew we were heading for marriage. I wanted to see what was out there. We never found anything we both liked. Then there was the fact that neither of us were sure where we wanted to live. We decided to take our time to find what we both wanted.

Once Crystal graduated, I thought things were going to slow down for her a little, but she took off like a rocket. She had the new salon and she went back to consulting other shops. She had taken a special interest in Kenny and Kim's place. They were in need of the help too.

They were in the middle of talks to bring Crystal in as a partner. I thought it was a great idea. Crystal and Kim get along great and Kenny loves anything that has to do with Crystal. Crystal even cut hair at their place twice a week, while training some of their girls.

My mother had been more than happy when she finally met Crystal. She loves her. According to my mother I should've proposed to Crystal at her graduation party. I just wasn't ready. Crystal had so much put together. I needed to have my head on straight when I did ask.

Since being in a relationship with Crystal, I'd almost carried my team to the super bowl. My value to the team had increased like crazy. Wanting to build a life with my girl made me more focused than I was before. I even decided to finish out my degree in the spring semester and not drag things out.

Six months and I don't have one complaint with our relationship. I'd been toying with the idea of proposing in September or October, around the time we first got together. Crystal had a few friends that had gotten engaged or married, also a few having babies. I saw how excited she got for them. I wanted that to be her.

It had been a long day in classes. I was glad for the off-season. I wanted to go home knowing I don't have to wake up early or think about anything but sleep. Crystal had the day off. I couldn't wait to get home to her.

We had plans to blend into the couch in front of the TV. I bought her favorite ice cream and picked up a few movies. I tried calling home, but she hadn't answered the phone and her cell kept going to voicemail.

I shook off the worry rising within. I figured she was probably sleeping, feeling as exhausted as I did. I didn't blame her for not wanting calls.

I was half way home when my phone started to ring. It was my mother. I got excited for the call. She was helping me plan something special for Crystal the following week. I'd hoped she had good news about the place I wanted to close out for the night.

"Hey, mom. What's up?" I crooned in the phone.

"Baby, you need to get home."

"What's wrong? Is Crystal alright?" I demanded.

Panic rose in my chest. Was Crystal not answering me because something was wrong with her? A million things began to run through my head.

"Something's going on. You need to get home now!"

"Mom, is she hurt?'"

"Lee, this is Kim," I heard another voice say into the phone. "I told you your mess was going to come back for you. Crystal is hysterical right now. You just need to get home."

I pulled into the garage as Kim spoke. Parking quickly, I noted that Crystal's car was there. I grabbed my things, running for the elevator. I had no idea what my mother or Kim were talking about.

"I'm getting in the elevator. I'll call you back," I grumbled into the phone.

The elevator ride felt like it was taking years. I played Kim's words over and over in my head. What could Crystal be hysterical about?

Things were going great between us. She knows I love her. I spend all my time with her when I'm not working or at school. I didn't understand where the problem was coming from.

I ran to the door and shoved my key in. When I opened the door, Crystal's bags were packed sitting beside the entrance. I felt my heart sink. What would make her want to leave? Was this about her not being able to stick to a relationship? I had so many questions.

We were good this morning. I barely made it out of the door. She clung to me as I debated going to class or staying home with her. At this point, it looked like I made the wrong choice. I should have stayed home.

I looked up to see Crystal sitting on the couch with her head in her hands. I didn't understand what was going on at all. It took me a second to realize there was someone else in the room. I still didn't focus on them, I couldn't pull my eyes off of Crystal.

I stepped into the apartment toward her, causing her to look up at me. I watched as she rose from her seat, walking over to me. She placed her hand on my stomach pressing a piece of paper against it. Standing on her toes to kiss me on the cheek. There were tears streaming down her cheeks and her hands were trembling.

"Baby, what's wrong?" I asked.

I reached to touch her face but she pushed my hand away. I watched in confusion as she moved around me, picking up her bags. I still didn't understand what was going on. I had dropped everything when I stepped through the door. The only thing left in my hand was the paper she handed to me. I wanted to look at it but I didn't want to take my attention away from her.

"Crystal, what's going on?" I barked out of frustration.

She didn't say a word, she just walked out of the door. I looked down at the piece of paper to see it wasn't a paper at all. It was a photo, a sonogram picture.

My first thought was that my girl was pregnant. Excitement coursed through my mind. Then, I realized she was too upset.

We'd talked about a family in the future. I knew she shouldn't have been this upset about it happening too early. Besides, I don't know much about this type of thing, but the baby in this sonogram was too developed to be in her stomach without me knowing.

That's when I remembered the other person in the room. They were still sitting behind me. They hadn't left out the door with Crystal. My heart told me to run after Crystal, but my thoughts told me I needed to know who was in my place. I turned around and saw it was a female sitting in the chair with her back to me.

"Excuse me. Can I help you?" I roared.

The woman stood up and turned toward me. My mouth dropped. It was Rachael. She was huge, her belly stuck out so far there was no question I was looking at her baby in the sonogram. I felt my heart squeeze.

"*Aw naw,*" I blurted out, turning to run for the door. "Crystal!"

I screamed her name as I ran out to find her. I had just missed her. The elevator closed as I made it to the hallway. I wanted to run for the stairs, but I wasn't leaving Rachael alone in my place for that long. Just look at what she had done. I haven't seen that girl in months. What was she doing here?

I took my phone out and tried dialing Crystal's phone as I walked back to the apartment. I slammed the door behind me and stood there with my hand on my temple. I tried to calm myself down. I wanted to scream and curse.

What the heck was going on?

"Rachael, can you explain what just happened?" I asked through my teeth.

"We're having a baby," she smiled.

"Are you nuts?"

"No. I wasn't sure I was going to tell you. I came looking for you today and she was here. I told her about us and about the baby and she got upset."

Her tome was so nonchalant as if she didn't just walk into my apartment and ruin my life. I could feel my blood boiling. My world was crumbling around me. I felt like I was standing in front of an oncoming train and couldn't jump out of the way.

"You told her about us? What *us*?" I growled.

"Maybe you need a minute. I'm a little hungry. Do you have something to eat?"

My phone rang before I could explode on her. I looked to see it was my mother. I picked up right away, she would know how to fix this. There had to be a way out of this twilight zone.

"Mom, Crystal's gone," I rushed into the phone.

"I bet she is. Is this girl really pregnant?"

"Yeah, it looks like it, but I can't say it's mine," I grumbled.

"Can you say it's not?" My mom yelled back.

"No. I mean, I used protection."

"And? Lee, I warned you. Kim warned you and I know Kenny warned you."

"Mom, I don't need to hear that right now. Crystal just left me. She wouldn't even talk to me."

"Honey, you gonna have to give that some time. Right now, you need to know if that baby is yours."

I sunk down to the floor and put my head in my hands. This wasn't happening to me. Not like this. I was losing the woman I wanted, the one I loved to something I wasn't sure was a fact.

My mother was right, they did warn me. This was the girl Kim was sure I needed to stay away from. Now, she was standing in the middle of my life like an ugly, *I told you so,* sign. I had just watched my future walk out of the door, along with my heart.

CHAPTER SEVENTEEN

Crystal Clear

Crystal

I guess I should pick up where Lee left off. But first, let me explain things from my side. I was in love with that man. I didn't think he could or would do any wrong. I would've done anything he asked me to.

However, when that girl showed up, I recognized her right away. She was the groupie from the club the night Lee asked me to come home with him. I knew he knew her.

I knew everyone knew her. I also knew her from when I used to party with my cousin, KG. She had been trying to trap someone for years. I was just furious that there was a chance she had trapped Lee. I wanted to believe he was smart enough not to have gotten caught up.

Let's be honest. Look at the drama he put me through, thinking I wanted to trap him. Something in my gut told me that sadly, Lee was that stupid. He had let the game play him and not played the game.

My father was the most disappointed, I believe. I think I saw his heart break twice, once for me and once for what he wanted for Lee. I just couldn't handle waiting to see if I had truly lost what I had allowed myself believed so much in. I ran home to my family and the comfort I knew.

It had been about eight months since I'd seen or talk to Lee. I heard he had a baby boy. Word is he's cute and has green eyes like his mother. Rachael had been living with Lee for about six months. Supposedly her roommate or whoever she was living with put her out.

Lee finally stopped calling me after three months, just before I decided to change my number. I changed it anyway because I didn't want the calls to start again. I just couldn't handle it. I was so heartbroken.

After that day she showed up at his place, I did what I do best. I threw myself into my work. I ran my salon in Westchester and I decided to go in as a partner with Kim and Kenny. We totally gutted the place and redid everything in their shop.

I also bought my second property and Craig was in the process of finishing another salon. I was determined to have some part of my life work out the way I wanted. It was the one area I had control over.

If only Craig would just do what I wanted in the first place, when I ask him to. As usual, we were arguing about the new shop. I needed to get out of there. The grand reopening for Kenny, Kim, and now my place, was in a few hours. Craig had done a great job redoing that place, but we fought the entire time as well.

"I don't see why I have to go through this. Just do what I ask," I sighed.

"If we put the booths in the way you're asking, it'll take up time and space. I think you can do this better."

That was Craig's problem he was always thinking. I don't pay him to rethink my ideas. I pay him to execute the ones I give him.

"I have how many salons? I consult for how many salons? I have given you business to how many salons? Are they not all successful?" I asked not hiding my irritation at all. "I think I know what works and I want it this way."

"Fine, Crystal, have it your way but when you call me back in to redo the place, I'm not giving you a discount," he grumbled.

"I didn't ask you for one."

"When are you two going to just get married?" Kenny chuckled, as he and Kim walked into the salon.

"And leave my quiet submissive wife? In your dreams," Craig chuckled.

"Whatever, Craig," I snapped. "Hey, you guys look great."

"Thank you very much. So do you," Kim sang, as she did a spin, then came over to hug me.

"Word, Ma, that dress is poppin'."

Kenny wiggled his eyebrows as he leaned in for a hug and pecked me on the cheek. Those two had become such good friends. Even with everything that happened between Lee and I, they never turned their backs on me.

"Thank you, Kenny," I giggled.

"So we get to meet this new boyfriend tonight, right?" Kim quizzed.

"Yes, and please be nice to him," I whined.

"We will be on our best behavior. Promise," Kenny crooned.

"Good," I beamed. "Okay, Craig. I think we've had enough arguing for today. I'll see you at the party."

"See you guys in a few," Craig grunted.

"Sounds like you want me to get a new contractor?"

"Crystal, I will see you in a few, my dear."

Craig plastered on the biggest smile I had ever seen. I walked for the door laughing and shaking my head at him. We fuss and all but he's the best at what he does.

I stopped just before we walked out the door to look in the mirror once more. After months of what I'd been through, I did look great. I had finally let Kim have her way. She dyed my hair a ruby red. I still wear my bangs sweeping across the front right side of my face, but I'd grown it out a little, letting the left side grow just above my ears.

I needed something different. I thought of it as sort of a cleansing to move forward. Things needed to change for my heart to start healing.

The white and peach dress that draped my body, cowled in the front. It dipped just below my bust line and haltered around my neck. The back of the dress was cut down to the waistline. Surely, my new boyfriend as Kim put it would love the look. He would have to because that was as much of a look as he was getting.

I reached into my peach bag for my lip gloss to freshen up my face. When I finished we were out the door. I walked to the parking lot with Kim and Kenny where I had a driver waiting for us. I knew they would be excited about my surprise, the reason I had them take a cab to come meet me instead of driving their cars.

"Word, Ma? A Bentley?" Kenny crooned as the waiting car came into view.

"Come on now. If I showed up for the opening of my other place in a Phantom, you know we were doing something sexy for this one," I sang as I slid into the car.

"That's my girl," Kim squealed.

Kenny got in after Kim, a frown marring his face. I wasn't sure what that was about. He went from one hundred to zero in the blink of an eye.

"Man, this makes what I'm about to say seem really messed up," Kenny mumbled.

"What, y'all changed y'all mind? You want to buy me out?" I chuckled.

"I wish that were it," Kim murmured.

"We kind of invited Lee," Kenny blurted out. "But Ma, listen, that's our boy. You know he's like our brother. We couldn't do something like this without him."

"Crystal, if it wasn't for him, we wouldn't know you," Kim almost whispered.

"Fine," I released a long deep sigh. "I don't have to like it, but he is your friend."

"Thanks, Crystal," they said in unison.

"You're not welcome." I said with a serious pout.

I didn't want to see, hear, or speak to Lee. I was so glad my parents were out of town for this. If I hadn't invited so many people, I would've skipped the whole thing. I already felt queasy. I spent the whole ride fidgeting with the split in the front of my dress.

We pulled up to the shop to an already growing crowd. I had some major PR done for this event. I was expecting it to be a great success.

We climbed out of the car to applause and cameras snapping. Things were falling into place just as I had planned them. The event was off to a great start.

The three of us walked inside to greet our guests that were already milling about. After making the rounds we took our stations by the entrance to greet those that would still be arriving. I was extremely happy with the turn out. We had a nice diverse crowd.

My date, Marcus, had arrived and was already mingling. I'd made sure to introduce him to Kim and Kenny. Kenny frowned at me as soon as Marcus wasn't paying attention.

Kim smiled while giggling to herself. I waited until we were all alone by the entrance to grill the two. It wasn't the reaction I was expecting from them.

"Okay, what was that?" I asked Kim.

"He's so not for you," she laughed out loud. "Fake Lee in the face."

"Whatever, Kim. He looks nothing like Lee," I grumbled.

"Sure, he isn't six foot something and built just like Lee. That brother is a light skin Lee if I ever saw one," she giggled.

"Shut up, Kim."

"I love you too, doll face."

"You're not funny."

I rolled my eyes at her. Only seconds later my heart stopped. Pain seared through my entire body.

In that same moment, Lee walked through the door looking like a chocolate god. I didn't think I would react like this to seeing him. I wanted to run to him and throw my arms around him. He looked great in his white suit and peach tie. I was happy I made it a white and peach affair. It looked great on him.

He was clean-shaven and his shape up looked like he'd just stepped out of the chair. I noticed he looked a little thinner than usual, but he was still built. Lee has always been too sexy for his own good, mine as well, for that matter. I don't understand why it is so hard for me to stay away from this man.

This is why I don't answer his calls and I refuse to talk to him. I lose all my good sense around him. That gorgeous face, with its perfect brown skin, jet-black eyebrows, and long thick eyelashes.

How could I resist? Just looking at him broke me down and sliced my heart in two. It was a physical ache that pulsed through me.

I watched as he gave Kenny five and a hug, exchanging a few words. Then he moved on to Kim, giving her a hug. He smile down at her as they talked and she fixed his tie. I didn't notice that I was biting my lip as I watched him, until he stopped in front of me. He leaned to kiss me on the cheek.

"Hey, Crystal, you look amazing," he beamed. "I love the new hair. That's what's up?"

"Hey Lee," I managed to say through my now dry mouth.

"I miss you." Lee's words hit me like a dagger.

"Hey, baby," Marcus crooned as he walked over.

He placed his arm around my waist, just before leaning to kiss the opposite cheek from the one Lee just kissed. His timing couldn't be worse, or maybe it was perfect. I felt my cheeks heat.

"Lee, I want you to meet Marcus," I said quickly. "Marcus, this is Lee."

"How you doing?" Marcus said as he held out his hand.

Lee looked like he just tasted something terrible. His face twisted in disgust as he held out his hand and shook Marcus's. It cut so deep to have Lee so close and want him so much.

I had to turn to look out toward the door. I couldn't allow him to see the look on my face. Though I could feel Lee studying with his penetrating gaze.

After a few seconds Lee turned, going to join some of the guests he knew. I tried my best to pull it together and breathe. I made it through the first hour, despite the feel of Lee watching my every move. It was driving me insane.

I tried to act normal. I threw myself into a conversation with Marcus and some of Kim's clients, but I was holding on by a thread. Every time Marcus placed his hands on me I wanted it to be Lee. Marcus would whisper in my ear and I would have to fight with myself not to cringe. I couldn't take it.

"Will you excuse me?" I said and turned to find Kim.

Those eyes were still watching me, but I wouldn't dare look his way. I needed to get out of there for a minute. I was going to lose it any second. I finally found Kim and grabbed her by the arm to pull her outside. When we got out front, I pulled her to the far left of the shop away from where the crowd of photographers and people dwindled.

The moment I knew we were free of all eyes and ears, I threw my face into her shoulder. I wrapped my arms around her and started crying. How could I want someone who hurt me so much? Why did I still love him?

This was so impossible. There I stood an educated, successful, and beautiful black woman. I didn't need to have Lee, but I wanted him. I wanted him more than anything.

Kim rocked me back and forth, rubbing my hair. I sobbed so hard chills ran up my back. My back stiffened and annoyance rose within when I felt hands rest on my waist. Marcus just didn't get it.

"Marcus, please just give me a minute," I sobbed.

"Nah, baby, my name ain't Marcus," I heard Lee whisper in my ear.

I turned to look at his face. He crushed his lips to mine. I didn't fight him. I wanted this, I wanted it badly. I missed him so much. I welcomed his hands on the small of my back. I couldn't help the moans escaping from me as he kissed me.

The photographers most have noticed Lee and I embracing. Cameras began to flash around us, capturing what should've been a private moment. I opened my eyes, breaking the kiss just in time to see Marcus walk out of the shop looking for me. The flashing cameras caught his attention. Immediately, a frown rushed across his face.

"Marcus, wait," I called as I pulled away from Lee.

Marcus had already started for the valet. I felt terrible. He was a nice guy. He just wasn't the one.

"Forget about him," Lee whispered in my ear, pulling my face back to his with his fingertips. "I love you, Crystal."

"I love you too, Lee."

I didn't mean to say it, but it's true. I was so unbelievably in love with him. I'd felt lost and like something was missing for months.

He wiped the tears from my eyes as he kissed me. I wanted to jump up and wrap my legs around him, but I fought the urge as much as I could. Just the fact that I hadn't let anyone get this close to me in eight months amplified the amazing feeling of being in his arms. It felt so good. After what seemed like a few minutes, Lee released me and pecked me on the cheek.

"Come on, you have a party to be at."

He grinned at me so confidently. It was one of the things that drew me to Lee, that smooth swagger he possessed. He moved like a man aware of himself and his power to make a woman's knees buckle.

I walked alongside him while he held his hand on the small of my back. It felt so right. I was meant to be at this man's side. I never loved any man the way I loved Lee.

I slid my arm around his back and he kissed the top of my head. As we returned to the party, Kim stood inside smiling like a little kid in an ice cream shop. I noticed Kenny nod at Lee in approval. I looked up to see a huge grin spread across Lee's lips. He looked much happier than he had when he arrived earlier.

Lee spent the rest of the night by my side. His hands remained in contact with me the whole time. It was easy to forget about everything we had been through to just have what I wanted for one night. He made me so happy.

When the party was over the cleaning crew showed up. Kim and Kenny stuck around with Lee and I to wait for the cleaners to finish up. We laughed and joked around just like old times. It felt good. I was finally able to breath.

Lee sat in one of the new barber chairs as I sat curled up on his lap. I totally ignored the fact that he was something I couldn't have.

Kim and Kenny decided to conveniently find something to do in the back room, as the cleanup crew started to move away from us. The moment they were gone, Lee began to caress my back, placing kisses against my neck. It felt amazing, but my brain told me to run.

"I miss you," he whispered in my ear.

"I miss you, too."

"I love you," he said in a gentle voice. "I've always loved you."

"Lee…I don't think we should do this. I miss you, but I," I tried to get out my reasons for not making this mistake, but before I could he had his juicy lips taking over my thoughts.

His hands squeezed at the bare skin of my back. I faded away from my sane thinking. The problem here was the fact that Lee knew I couldn't tell him no. He knew the moment he walked in that door tonight he could have me anyway he wanted. Some part of me would always be his, no matter how much that part hurt me.

"I want you," he moaned.

"Mmmm, no."

"Please, Crystal, I miss you. I want you."

"No, Lee." I tried to hold onto my resolve.

I couldn't just cave. I have to hold onto my will. It would be so much easier if I would get up and walk away, but silly me, I sat there letting him kiss me.

"Crystal, I love you. Please, baby, you know you want to. I miss you. Let me have you," he breathed in my ear. "Let daddy take care of you."

"Please, don't do that."

"Why not? I want you. Say yes."

"Lee," I groaned.

"Crystal, say yes."

"Yes, baby, yes." What was the use? I gave in and kissed him. "You'll come home with me?"

"Yeah, baby."

"Okay."

I should have been ashamed of myself, but I wasn't. I knew this man was my weakness. He ruined me long ago.

I had just bought a place of my own a month ago. I didn't want him to drive there so I talked him into riding in the rental with me. Kenny agreed to take his car for him. Once that was settled we were in the rental with the driver, heading to my place.

This was only making this worse by the minute. The more he touched me, the more he kissed me, the more I smelled his cologne, the deeper into trouble I got myself. I would regret it all later. I couldn't help myself though. I truly did love him and I missed him so much.

When we got to my house we barely made it through the door. I tried to get him to my bedroom but that wasn't happening. Not at first at least.

Lee tore at my dress, leaving it in a tatter heap at my feet. We both peeled him from his clothes, tossing them all over my living room, only stopping for him to pull protection from his wallet. When we were both stripped bare, Lee wrapped his arm around my waist, lifting me onto him.

I wrapped my legs around him, looking into his eyes. He cupped my face brushing his thumb across my lips. All the emotions I'd tried to bury surfaced.

"You're more beautiful than I remember. I need you so much," he said softly.

"What are you waiting for," I replied.

A smile took over his lips as he reached between us, guiding himself into me. My lids half closed, my teeth clenched. I had to suck the drool back into my mouth. It was that good.

"Damn, you so tight. You ain't give my pussy away, did you?" his strained words washed over me.

"Never," I moaned.

He took my lips as his hands cupped my backside and guided me up and down on him. His stance widened so he could thrust deeper. My head dropped to his shoulder.

He moved to the couch to balance me on the back. My legs went to his shoulders as he shifted me. I grabbed the back of the couch. His hand covered one of mine, his other holding one of my legs to his chest.

The couch rocked with his thrusts. His arms had to shoot out to wrap around me to keep me from falling back as he pounded into me not letting up for a second. We were defying gravity.

"Yes, Lee, yes," I cried. "Oh yes."

"Play with that pussy for me," I looked at him, afraid the move would topple me. "Don't worry, I got you. I always got you."

I nodded, panting and sweating already. I lifted my fingers to my mouth to wet my fingertips. Reaching between us, I found my nub and started to rub it.

"Yes," he hissed between his teeth.

A vein popped in the side of his neck. He was wrecking me. My eyes rolled to the back of my head. I don't know how I'd survived without this in the last few months.

My kitty sucked at him like she was starved. I was so close I knew I was going to go over the next time he brushed that perfect spot. That's exactly what happened.

He looked into my eyes and intentionally angled to tap at the point of detonation. He earned the rapid multiple explosions he wrung from my body.

"Shit," I screamed.

He followed me over not too long after. His chest pressed to mine as he released my legs to let them dangle at his sides. I wrapped my arms around his back.

"Damn, I missed you so much," he breathed into my hair. "Don't move. I just need to hold you for a minute."

I remained silent. So many things were running through my head. I allowed my breathing to return to normal as my sanity tried to make a return.

Lee's warm lips on the side of my neck blew that plan out of the water. My doubts were obliterated with each soft kiss. We made it to my room eventually, after he was satisfied enough to let me get up as he followed me.

For the first time since I walked away from him, I fell asleep peacefully in his arms. I had no idea how much I missed that. I got the impression that he missed me as much as I missed him. He woke me up in the middle of the night to show me just how much he did, over and over again. I didn't mind, I missed him that much too.

CHAPTER EIGHTEEN

Can I Do This?

I had so much to do that next day, but I woke up a little late. I woke to Lee lying next to me staring at my face. I couldn't help the huge grin that spread across my lips.

"Good morning," he said, kissing my forehead.

His breath smelled like toothpaste. I was so not talking to him. I waved at him before rolling to go brush my teeth. He reached for my waist, pulling me back to him.

"I'll be right back," I murmured as I covered my mouth and giggled.

"Hurry up."

I went into the bathroom with my huge smile still intact, until I made it to look in the mirror. Being able to see myself in the mirror made me ask myself some serious questions. Like what was I doing? Did I think I could be happy like this? Did I think I could have him?

A fool stared back at me in the mirror. The stupid grin on her face should have choked her. Anger started to rise inside me again. All of the feelings that coursed through the day Rachael arrived started to surface.

A tear fell from my eye, pouring out not even a fraction of the pain. I ran the water to wash my face. As I brushed my teeth, I wished I had just walked away from him last night. If I had it wouldn't hurt so much this morning, and why had I let him come home with me. To my new home, my new bedroom. I would always have the memory of last night in this house.

I slowly made my way back to the bedroom. I went to sit on the edge of the bed, but he pulled me to him. His eyes searched my face as a worried look took over his face.

"What's wrong?" he asked.

"This is wrong. I can't have you. Why did I let you come home with me?"

"Baby, please…don't do this. I need you. I love you, Crystal. We belong together."

"She lives with you?"

"Yeah, but I'll go get a place today. If that's what you want. I can stay in a hotel or get an apartment somewhere," he offered anxiously. "She doesn't have a place to go and I can't have my little man on the street, but I can move out."

"But I don't want that. You should be with your son."

I'd already thought about all of this before. I knew what I couldn't ask him to do. I'd played the scenarios over and over in a million different ways.

"Baby, if that's the case I'll take him with me. Trust me that's not a problem."

"No, that's his mother. You can't take her son from her. He needs his mother."

"Please," he snorted.

"See, I'm not getting in the middle of that," I grumbled.

"You are not getting in the middle of anything. I've been thinking about moving out or something already. Last night was the best I've slept in months. Rachael doesn't do anything but stress me out."

He looked stressed just talking about it. I wanted to sympathize with him. It just wasn't coming easy.

"You're sleeping with her."

It was sort of an accusation and statement at the same time. My chest burned as I waited for his reply. I didn't want to know, but I also needed to know.

"No."

"I'm not going to do this. You live in a one-bedroom condo, I know she's sleeping in your bed with you and I know you are sleeping with her. If you don't want to tell me the truth then we can forget this."

"Yeah, I was. I mean, we slept in the same bed but I haven't touched her in a minute." His tone was sincere. It cut me deeply to know he had been with her again. "Crystal, it's not like that with her. All she does is drive me crazy."

"I don't know."

"I've got all day. We can figure this out, but I need you," he pleaded. "I know we can figure this out."

"I have so much to do today. I have the new shop and Craig is driving me nuts. I have appointments I need to go to."

"I can come with you. I need to figure out how to get you back."

His brown eyes were so serious. The tension in his face was palpable. His face was so intense. The profound need I saw in their depths reached beyond the physical need we fulfilled last night.

"Okay," I sighed. "I need to get dressed. I should be out the door already."

I got up and started to get ready. I had a million voices in my head telling me this was wrong. I did my best to get ready and ignore the screaming thoughts within. Once I was dressed, I found Lee redressed in his dress shirt and suit pants from the night before. He still looked more handsome than necessary.

"Would it be okay if I go to my place to change?" he asked.

"I'm already late," I shrugged and laughed nervously.

Moving outside we jumped into my lotus, my father's gift for me sticking to and finishing graduate school. I laughed to myself as I thought about Lee's reaction to my other car. I had plenty of nice cars. It'd always been one of the ways my father spoiled me.

It was kind of hard for me to drive to Lee's place. I hadn't been there since I went for the last of my things. That last trip had nearly torn me apart.

Lee spent the entire ride staring at me, reaching to brush his hand against my face repeatedly. It was all so comforting. I wanted to figure things out between us, I just didn't know what I was getting myself into.

As I pulled into the garage my chest became super tight. I parked the car and turned it off, taking a deep breath. Lee leaned over to kiss my cheek, then turned my face to face him so he could capture my lips in a soul-searing kiss.

"Come on," he said softly.

"Oh, I'm not going up there," I rushed.

"Why not?"

"She is there isn't she?" I asked.

"Yeah and?"

"I don't think that is a good idea."

I think Lee was losing it. I didn't belong in the same room as that girl. I didn't need that kind of drama. He could have all of that.

"That's still my place. Let's go," he demanded.

"Lee."

"Let's go, Crystal."

He got out of the car and I slowly followed him out. I knew this was a bad idea, but once again, I wasn't following what I knew. I was following what Lee wanted.

He wrapped his arm around my waist, leading me to the elevator. On the ride up he stared into my eyes, swaying me in his hold. I love his coffee brown eyes. They're amazing with their deep-set almond shape.

When we got off the elevator, it was like in the movies when you can hear the actor breathing as they walk down the hallway to their doom. Lee held me tightly, which allowed me to relax a little. My nerves shot through the roof when he turned the key in the door.

Pushing the door open revealed her standing there holding their baby. My heart squeezed in my chest. Her face turned into a frown the moment she saw me. I felt the same way about her if she wanted to know the truth. I wanted to hit Lee in the back of the head.

"Why didn't you come home last night?" she whined in an irritating voice.

"Because I was minding my own business," Lee answered with a hard edge in his voice.

"Lee needed you," she insisted.

Lee pursed his lips and rolled his eyes at her. He tossed his suit jacket down and reached for the baby. Once he was in his arms, it felt like the wind was knocked out of me. He looked just like Lee. Only difference was the green eyes. I closed my lids tightly trying not to think. All hope that this would all just go away was lost. That little boy was Lee's without question.

"Hey, little man. Is your mother telling the truth? You needed me?" He cooed at the baby.

I opened my eyes to see Lee pursed his lips again.

"Just like I thought. You were cool all night."

He kissed the top of the baby's head, while rubbing his back. This was too much for me. I felt sick. I tried to think of a way out.

"May I use the bathroom?"

The question was the first thing that popped into my head. I needed a moment to breathe. I had to get away from this scene.

"Sure."

Lee reached for my hand and walked me up the hallway as if I could have possibly forgotten where to find the bathroom for myself. I could feel his eyes on me. He was watching me intently. Like watching a scared animal to see if they would lash out and attack.

I rushed in the bathroom and closed the door. Putting the lid down on the toilet, I took a seat to clear my head. My head fell into my palms as I questioned myself.

Why am I here?

I was such a fool. Was there even enough love in the world for me to get through this? And to make it worse, I could hear them starting to argue through the walls.

"How you gonna bring her up in here?" I heard her yell.

"What? Rachael, are you crazy? I'll bring anyone I want up in here. This is my crib. You remember you're still a guest," he bellowed.

"You straight disrespecting me, bringing her in here."

"You trippin'. You're not my girl. I told you to get yourself together and get out months ago."

"You not tryin' to give me money to get someone to watch Lee."

"I told you. I'm not giving you no money. You got somebody to watch him, I want to meet them. Then they need to let me know the fee. But you need to go, for real."

"Whatever, this isn't about me. Why you bring her up in here?"

"First of all, you need to bring your tone down. If it wasn't for you and that condom that supposedly, so conveniently broke. I would be engaged to *her* and about to marry *her* not standing here arguing with you."

With those words my world fell apart. I knew Lee wanted to marry me, but hearing him say it hurt so much. I had to get out. I didn't want to see or hear anymore.

I slid off my heels and stood to creep to the door. I inched the door opened and peeked out. It sounded like they were in the bedroom, but I wanted to be sure. When the coast was clear I made a run for it.

Thank goodness for track in high school. I didn't take one look back. I was out of the apartment and on the stairs, sprinting for my car.

I prayed Lee didn't see me fly pass. I'm fast but so is he and he's in shape to run after me. I ran like I stole something. When I hit the parking lot, I didn't even stop to put my shoes back on. I jumped in my car and peeled out.

Once I was out of the lot, I knew I was safe. Kenny must have still had Lee's car. It wasn't in the garage, which reassured me that Lee couldn't follow me. He couldn't call me either. I hadn't given him my number.

I could feel the tears warm my cheeks. I knew all this was stupid. It was juvenile behavior that was so out of pocket for me.

I went right to where my day should've started. I hoped Craig would see today wasn't a day to fight with me. I needed to forget last night. I wanted to forget about today too.

I maneuvered into the parking lot and cried myself out. I needed to get it all out before I could go inside. I found some tissue in my purse and cleaned my face. I looked in the mirror at the hot mess I'd become. I promised myself this wouldn't be me again. Why was this happening?

I took a deep breath and made my way into the salon. Finding a pair of shades in my bag, I tossed them on to cover my swollen eyes. I moved on autopilot.

I almost collapsed when I entered the salon. I stepped right into a puddle of water. My brand new hardwood floors were covered in water. I felt the rage rock through me. Craig stumbled towards me looking as if he were about to explain.

"Craig, I don't care! I don't need this right now. I know this was your guys. You fix this. Fix it now and it's coming out of your pockets!" I screamed and turned to leave.

I made it back to the car, consumed in tears before I could get inside. My cell began to ring, drawing my attention. I prayed it wasn't more bad news. Relief filled me as soon as I saw Kim's name on the screen. I needed to talk to her.

"Hello."

"Honey, what's going on? Lee called Kenny upset and Kenny called me having a fit," she started.

"I can't …I can't be with him. That little boy looks just like him. It's not fair, Kim. I wanted to be the one to give him babies. That was supposed to be my son. It hurts so much. I love him, why is this happening? The worst part is I did the math. She got pregnant when we first got together. That was almost my baby. I just missed giving him his first son."

I sobbed out of control. The pain nearly choking off my air supply. It stung like a deathly venom rushing my veins.

I was completely thrown by the voice I heard next. I hadn't understood that Kim had me on three way. My stomach was turning and nearly pitched.

"You think I don't think about that," Lee yelled into the phone. "You think I don't wish it was your eyes I see every time I look at him. You think I don't wish he was yours. Crystal, that makes me sick. It makes me sick that it's not you that gave me my first baby, all my babies. Baby, I messed up and I can't take it back, but I love you. Just tell me where you are."

"No, I can't."

"Please, where are you?" he demanded.

"I'm not doing this."

"Crystal, where are you?"

I hung up the phone and got into my car. I wasn't going to be any good to anyone today. I called my assistant and cancelled my whole day. I was going home to sleep the entire nightmare off.

I got home and showered, put on a t-shirt, and curled up into my bed. The moment my head hit the pillow, I knew that was a mistake. My sheets smelled just like him.

I balled up in the middle of the bed and started to cry. I cried for at least two hours when it registered that someone had started to ring the doorbell.

I wished they would go away. The few people that knew I lived here would only stand there and tell me, *I could have told you so*. I didn't need to hear that crap.

Whoever it was wouldn't go away. I knew I should've pulled into the garage. Seeing my car in the driveway had to be the reason for their persistence.

After twenty minutes of the bell ringing, I was totally annoyed. My parents were due back this afternoon, but they would call. If it was Ricky I was going to kick his tail.

I opened the door to see the one person I didn't want to see. I knew picking a door with glass too high for me to see out of was going to be a problem. I went to slam it back, but he pushed his way in. He grabbed me, pulling me onto his waist. He kicked the door closed behind him. I was stunned as he marched straight for my bedroom.

"I love you," he breathed into my face. "If you want my baby, I'll give you one. I can't lose you."

"Lee, stop," I sobbed. "Please, this hurts too much."

"It doesn't have to. I love you, my son doesn't change that."

He carried me all the way into my bedroom and laid me down on the bed. He reached down, pulling his shirt over his head. My mouth popped open when I comprehended his intention.

He was serious. He was going to try to get me pregnant. I knew he had lost his damn mind. I turned and crawled to the far corner of the bed away from him. Grabbing a pillow, I held it to my chest like a safety guard between us.

"You getting me pregnant doesn't fix this," I shouted at him.

"Then what will, Crystal? What will show you I love you and you're what I want?"

"Don't do this. Just let me get over you and move on."

"No, I can't. Just like you can't. We haven't been together in how long? And you still love me. Let me fix this. Let me love you."

"It hurts," I sobbed.

"Come here, baby. It doesn't have to. Let me fix it."

I slowly put the pillow aside, crawling back over to him. I wrapped my arms around his back and cried into his bare chest. He hugged me so tight, I felt like I couldn't breathe. I wanted him to fix this. I wanted to try. I wouldn't let him get me pregnant, but somehow we would find a way.

Climbing onto my bed and puling me onto his chest, he let me sob for hours while he rubbed my back. I ignored my ringing phone and the outside world, allowing him to make it better. Just having his arms around me was a start. He didn't say a word and he didn't have to.

I don't remember when, but at some point I fell asleep. When I woke Lee was still holding me, but he was knocked out. He looked so peaceful. That turned my thoughts to something he'd said. He hadn't slept in months. Football season was back on. He couldn't function like that.

It also nagged at me that he did look thinner. Lee didn't look like he was taking care of himself. That worried me. I wasn't sure if he needed sleep or food more. He was sound asleep so I got up to make him something to eat for when he woke up.

I already had meat down in the refrigerator to make myself some spaghetti. I cooked that up quickly and hunted through the freezer for some vegetables. I made some green beans, which were his favorite. I decided to also make some corn on the cob. I wanted to have as much food on his plate as I could.

He woke up like clockwork. I'd just finished up when he came out of the bedroom stretching and yawning. I smiled at him, pointing to the table for him to take a seat. He smiled rubbing his stomach, taking the seat closest to him as he moved to the table. I took a huge plate of food over to him. I had even made him some garlic bread.

He pulled me to him to kiss me soundly on the lips. Warmth spread through me reminding of how simple things used to be. I missed that simplicity.

"Thank you."

"You're welcome, baby. Can I ask you something?"

"Yeah," he answered after blessing his plate and starting to tuck in.

"You look thin. Is your chef not taking care of you?"

He snorted at me, but continued to eat. My brows knotted at his response.

"True story. Rachael made Manny quit. I've been living off takeout and junk food, when I don't crash at Corey or Brantley's."

"You're kidding, right?"

A deep frown consumed my face. I couldn't believe what I was hearing. The look on Lee's face said he was containing his own rage.

"You think I'm kidding. I told you I don't sleep. I'm too stressed to sleep."

"I don't understand. How are you supposed to play like this?"

"I don't want to talk about that," he grumbled.

"What about school? Did you finish?"

I wanted to know what else was lacking since I left his life. This was pure insanity. Lee was on track to do amazing things when we were together. I couldn't even wrap my head around this.

"Yeah, I finished. I just haven't done anything else."

"Baby, if it's that bad you can stay here. At least, until you figure things out," I offered.

"Are you sure? You don't know how much I need that. I've been looking at places. My mom just doesn't want me to leave Rachael in my condo. She made me have Rachael send all her mail to a PO Box. She told me not to give her a key either. I pay the doormen to let her in and out. That right there be causing me to lose sleep. You know Larry and Fred are cool, but I don't like the idea that I got to trust them with the keys to my crib."

He looked stressed out with every word he spoke. My head was spinning. This was too much.

"Yeah, I'm sure," I answered placing my hand on his face. I could even see the weight loss there. "Eat up so you can shower and get some more sleep."

I still knew his schedule. I was sure he had practice the next day. I wanted him to get some real rest. He didn't have to worry about me. I was going to take care of him. I was one less thing he didn't have to worry about.

CHAPTER NINETEEN

A Plan

Lee woke up the next morning to a huge breakfast. I made him French toast, eggs, sausage, turkey bacon, a half a grapefruit and a huge glass of apple juice. He looked so happy. I had a full day ahead of me, but he needed to be taken care of first.

I tried to wrap up my day early so I could get home to let him in and get dinner started. When I pulled into the driveway I found Lee fast asleep in his car. I felt so bad, I didn't want to wake him but he needed to get into the bed.

The unnatural way he was curled up was crazy for a man his size. Even being in a bigger car now, an E350, instead of his Porsche, it looked ridiculous. It was only about three in the afternoon, but he looked like he could use a few more hours or just call it a day to sleep his way through the night.

"Baby," I called tapping on his driver's side window as I peer through the glass.

The moment those brown eyes opened slowly my heart squeezed in my chest. Lee is just a beautiful man. There was no arguing about it, I didn't want anyone else's opinion. I knew what the man did to me. I was under his spell before he even knew. The first time I saw him I stopped in my tracks and forgot what the hell I was doing.

He clearly looked confused at first. It took a moment for his eyes to focus before he looked around him while straightening in his seat. He opened to door and slowly unfolded his large frame from the vehicle. My insides warmed as he towered over me. I loved the feeling of being engulfed in his presence. His all-consuming aura wrapped me in a sense of safety.

He kissed the top of my head, while pulling me into a bear hug. Wrapping my arms around him felt like returning home after the worst week ever. We stood there for a moment before he led me to the back of his car.

I'd be lying if I said I didn't get excited when he pulled his luggage out of the trunk. I helped him make his way into the house, holding his small laptop bag. When we pushed our way inside he seemed to wake up a bit, pulling me to the couch with him to relax.

Once we were seated he placed his face into my belly taking a deep breath. I felt his entire body relax as I began to I rub his head. Those silky waves smooth to the touch, always fresh and spinning.

"What's going on with your barbershop?" I quizzed.

Last we were together he talked of opening a barbershop. Not a unisex place like mine and his friend's. He wanted a place just for men. I understood that. It was his wheelhouse. He wanted a sporty lounge type of feel in his place.

"I don't have time for that. I haven't been focused on it. I would love to have it poppin' right now. Something else for me to do." He sighed, tiredly.

"I have an idea. I'm looking at my next location, it's a five unit storefront. The owner is selling them separately, but I want them all and I think I can get a great price. You can look at it. If you like the place, you can put in the percentage for the unit and I'll give you the deed on it," I offered.

I had been thinking about him and his goals all day. He had undeniably lost focus. I could see that light missing from his eyes.

"For real, I'm real interested in that," he lifted his face, his eyes locked with mine as they glowed anew.

"Are you too tired? I can see if we can look at it tonight."

"No, I'm ready."

It was obvious he'd caught his second wind. I could feel the excited energy coming off of him. He was absolutely wide-awake now.

"Okay, I'll call my agent and see if I can get an appointment for tonight."

I picked up my phone to make the call. As I dialed his phone started to ring. I watched as he looked at the phone, a scowl appearing on his handsome face. I knew exactly who it was, I didn't have to think twice or ask. He answered his phone, grumbling into it through tight lips.

"Hello, Jamie," I called into my phone as my realtor answered.

"Hey Crystal, how can I help you today?" she sang back to me.

"I want to show that multi-unit to a potential partner. Can we see it today?" Lee waved his hand at me. "Oh, wait, Jamie."

"I have to go get my son," Lee grumbled.

"So you want to go tomorrow?" I asked.

"No, I just need two hours. Give me the address, I'll meet you there."

"Okay," I nodded at him. "Jamie can we meet in two hours?"

"Sure honey, you know the place. We'll meet in two hours," Jamie chimed.

I hung up the phone. Lee's jaw was clenched so tight I thought it would break. I didn't want to pry into his business with Rachael, but he looked so upset. I waited to see if he would tell me on his own.

"It won't take me long," he grumbled.

"Okay, do we need to be done by a certain time to get him back to his mom?"

He snorted, making a sour face. The look of disgust was tangible, I could almost taste something sour in my own mouth. I tried to push that down and listen without judging.

"Nah, she said she has an emergency, which means she ain't coming back for a few days. Ain't nothing new."

"Oh."

My head whipped back. That little boy hadn't turned one yet. To think that his mother would disappear like she didn't have him to take care of turned my stomach, but again I tamped down my thoughts and emotions. I had to set myself some boundaries here.

"Let me go get my little man. I'll meet you in two hours," he stood up, bending to kiss me before he left.

Panic seized me. I don't have anything in my house for a baby. Where would he sleep? He needed toys, food, and pampers. I had none of that.

I called Kim right away. I knew she had babysat for Lee a few times. She would know what I needed. I had a room for him. My house had four bedrooms and the one right next to mine just happened to be empty. It's the other two rooms that were still acting as storage until I found time to unpack.

"Hey girl," Kim answered her phone.

"Kim, I need your help," I rushed.

"Everything okay?" she asked nervously.

"Yeah, It's just, Lee has to keep the baby. I don't have baby things here. Can you and Kenny meet me at Babies Station? I need Kenny's truck and maybe your car. I don't have long."

"We're on it. Text me the one you're on your way to and we'll be there," she chimed through the phone.

"Okay, thank you so much."

I grabbed my bag and ran out to the car. I texted her the address as I rushed to get there. I needed so much. I gunned my way to the store as fast as I could.

I picked a location in between my house and Kim and Kenny. I stopped only to run into the hardware store to make Lee a copy of my house keys and an extra set to give to Kim and Kenny so they could take the things to my place for me, while I met up with Lee. When I arrived at Baby Station they were in the lot waiting for me.

"Hey Ma," Kenny called as I rushed out of the car.

"Hey guys, thank you so much. I need a crib, baby tub, swing. Oh my gosh, I need everything."

"Calm down, Crystal. We'll take care of little man," Kim soothed.

I took a deep breath, grabbing a cart while motioning for them both to do the same. I moved as fast as I could. I had baby detergent, body wash, lotion, wash clothes, bottles, a sterilizer, I even picked up locks for the cabinets for when he got bigger.

When I was done with the small stuff, we went to look for a crib. I picked a gorgeous crib and I had to have the rocker to match. I could just see Lee with his son in his arms, rocking him to sleep. Lee seemed so good with him.

I got the matching changing table and dressers. I wanted him to have a full room. I bought clothes, a swing, and tons of toys. It was crazy how much we had. I looked at my watch and groaned. I was running late. We rushed to the counter. I grumbled to myself as I prayed the girl at the register would wake up and move faster.

My phone started to ring just as I swiped my card to pay. I knew it was Lee. I hoped the baby wasn't fussy because he had to sit in the car waiting for me.

"Hey, baby," I called into the phone.

"Hey, is everything okay?" he asked nervously.

"Yeah, I just needed to take care of something. I'm on my way right now."

"Okay, don't rush. Take your time," he said with concern.

"I'll be fine. See you in a few."

I hung up the phone and started to push my cart out. I tried to help get the things in the cars. We had so much.

"Oh no," I whined. "We got everything but baby food. Crap."

"Relax, we got this. Go meet Lee. Kim can watch little man later while y'all hit the grocery store. You got those keys for us," Kenny said holding out his hand.

"Okay, here," I nodded, reaching in my bag for the key and handing it over. "His room is the second bedroom on the left."

"*His* room," Kim squealed.

I rolled my eyes, but turned to run and jump in my car. I raced off to meet Lee, sending Jamie a text to tell her I was on the way. It took me about twenty minutes to get to them. I felt so bad they had to wait so long, especially the baby. I parked in the first spot I could find.

Jumping out of the car, I rushed over to Jamie. She knows I'm never late. Thank goodness she still looked happy to see me. She knows she's in for a commission so I'm sure she would've waited two more hours.

"Hey, Jamie," I chimed as I kissed her on each cheek.

"Hey honey, you look great as usual," Jaime chimed back.

"You too girl."

"Hey," Lee said as he walked up with his son in his arms. He watched my face closely, searching my reaction.

"Hey," I said, lifting on my toes to kiss him on the cheek. "Jamie, this is Lee. Lee, this is Jamie."

"Nice to meet you, Lee."

"Nice to meet you, too."

I looked at Lee's son as he rested against his father's shoulder. I felt a small tug in my chest. I don't know what possessed me to speak the next words that came out of my mouth.

"Can I hold him?" I asked.

Lee looked surprised at my request, but handed the baby over. He came right to me. Boy, he was a solid baby. I shifted his weight so I could have a good hold on him.

Jamie led us to the first unit on the corner. I was excited. I seriously wanted this property, it had so much potential. Lee smiled as we walked, his hand on my back. Little Lee babbled in my arms as he played with the necklace around my neck. It was a gift from his father to me. A diamond heart pendant that I still wore every day. We walked into the first unit and I looked up at Lee. His face lit up as he took it all in.

"I want to make this a beauty supply. It can supply the salon and the barber shop," I explained.

"I can see that. Raise a platform there for the register, the hair extensions over there, the products and extras running up that way," he mused.

"Exactly," I grinned. Lee described exactly what I had envisioned. "The storage room is huge. Go take a look. I don't want to take the baby back there."

Jamie took Lee back to the storage room while giving him details on square footage. I stood with the baby swaying back and forth. He was such a quiet baby.

I looked down to find it was because he'd fallen asleep against my chest looking just like Lee. I closed my eyes to take a minute to deal with who's child I was holding. A tear escaped, but I quickly wiped it away.

I think Lee saw it. When he and Jamie returned to me he wrapped his arms around me, holding me tightly. He kissed the top of my head, rubbing up and down my arm. He pressed his face to the side of my temple as Jamie talked more about the unit.

We moved to the next one allowing me to regain my composure. We walked in and I looked up once again to check Lee's reaction. He smiled again scanning the space.

"This one will be the service salon and my first official teaching location. Karen is working on the process for me," I chimed.

"This place is huge," Lee crooned.

"Yup and this is going to be full service. There's room for a washer and dryer for the towels. Over there will be the nails and in the back there will be a mud room, lashes and brows, full range of wax treatments and I'm looking into bringing in this girl that does stuff like chemical peels. You know?"

"That's hot."

Lee looked around like he could see everything I explained. Jamie sold her heart out, giving Lee the grand tour and benefits of the location. I just stood, watching him take it all in. I'd even settled into holding onto the baby. It was funny how comfortable I'd gotten so fast.

Jamie wrapped up with showing Lee the back room and the outdoor loading area. We left out for the next unit, which I was excited to show him. It would be the unit I wanted Lee to consider for his barbershop.

We walked in and my eyes were glued on him. His eyes were scanning again, as he nodded to himself. I felt like I was busting at the seams. I wanted him to like the place. I wanted to help him get it running. Craig had work for the next year with all the plans I had.

"This is the unit I was thinking of for you. I thought you could have your chairs on this wall and set up flat screens on this wall. Maybe a few overhead, facing this way for those waiting or you can go with the larger mirrors that will reflect them. There's a nice office in the back of this suite," I started.

"Yeah, I was thinking the same thing. This spot is golden, baby. Man, I'm feeling this."

His determination was back. I could see my Lee, the ambitious one. I stood quietly for a minute to let him think and soak it all in.

"Do you like it?"

"Yeah, I have mad ideas."

His face was so intense. I could see the calculating and planning in his eyes. This was the man I'd first met, the one with a plan for his life and future.

"I want to put a gym and a clothing store in the other two units. My brother Henry's wife is launching her line and I think it's going to take off. We were talking about her doing a boutique. I know I can drive the right traffic here."

"I'm with it. I mean I know you just want me to pay for the barbershop, but I want to put in more." He shrugged his shoulders, turning to look into my eyes. "I want to go in half, if that's cool with you."

"I guess. I mean, if you're sure you're ready for that. I was planning to make an offer this week."

Taking a small mental step back. I thought about what he was truly asking me. I was okay with starting a business with Lee. I knew he was smart and we totally thought a lot alike when it came to business. I could handle that.

"I'm ready. I need this right now. I need to get back on track."

"Okay, Jamie, do you have the paperwork we were talking about? I would like to show Lee what I am willing to offer."

"You know I am always ready for you, girl," Jamie sang.

"Okay, let's go see the last two units and we can talk."

My business hat was on now that Lee wanted to get serious about this. I knew it and was used to it. When it came time to get things done, I zone in on the task.

We looked at the last two units. Lee flipped over the size of the unit for the gym. I could see the excitement coursing through him. It was a great location and we would be able to work the area for maximum traffic and flow.

We discussed the numbers back outside. Lee was floored by the steal we were getting, the owner was extremely motivated. I still wasn't going to offer asking price, but I was sure we would close for what I wanted. If I know anything as well as I know hair and salons, it's real estate and how to strike while the iron is hot.

We wrapped up with Jamie officially putting the offer on the table. Starting for the cars, I realized I was still holding the baby. He started to get a little heavy as I looked down into his sleeping face, but I didn't want to disturb his nap by handing him to Lee. When we got to the car, Lee reached for his son hugging him to his chest. I watched as he pressed his face to the baby's head, staring at me over the wooly locks on top of his son's crown.

"Call you later?" Lee asked looking like someone stole his best friend.

My brows knotted in confusion. I searched his face to figure out what he was thinking. The sadness in his eyes twisted at my heart.

"What do you mean?"

"I don't know when she's coming back for him. When she does this, she disappears for days or weeks at a time. I want to call you later and talk," he explained.

"You're not coming home?" I almost whispered, disappointment lacing my words.

"I didn't think you wanted me there with him. I don't want to hurt you."

"If you're staying with me he's welcome in my home. He belongs where you are. He's yours. I want him there if I want you there. I want you to come home."

"Are you sure?" he said with a slight smile pressing at the corners of his mouth.

"Yes. Let's get him home."

Lee stepped toward me, dipping his head to kiss me. It was a tender kiss. One that spoke of appreciation and care.

"I love you."

I looked into his eyes and there it was. The love that was meant for me, the look that said what I didn't need words to hear. It was what I always wanted from the man in my life.

"I love you too."

Lee placed the baby in his car seat and strapped him in as I stood watching. When he finished he got in his car and waited for me to get in mine. We were off to my place once I pulled out of the spot. I hoped that Kim and Kenny got some of the stuff put together.

When we arrived at my house, I pulled in and let Lee park behind me. I noticed Kenny and Kim had parked out front. I rushed out of my car to go help Lee with the baby. He looked so stressed out all over again. I couldn't help wondering if Rachael had called him with some more mess.

"Everything okay?" I asked as I reached for the diaper bag.

"I need to run and get a playpen or something for him to sleep in and some food and stuff," he thought out loud. "I don't want to ask you to watch him. I should have just gone before we got here."

"Lee, don't worry about that," I beamed. "I can run to get him some food."

"I can't ask you to share your bed with both of us."

"Lee, it's me. Let me take care of you. I got this."

I couldn't wait to show him what I'd done. I wanted him to see that I thought of him and his son. I could do this.

I took him by the hand, leading him into the house. Kim and Kenny sat in the living room opening toys and other things

I'd bought. They were placing them all in organizers. It was clear that Kim stopped to do more shopping.

I looked up at Lee to gauge his reaction. Shock was written all over his face. Baby stuff littered my home covering every surface.

Understanding registered on Lee's face, he now knew what I had done, how I'd taken care of him and his son. He turned to look at me. For the first time since I've known him I saw tears gather in his eyes. I thought for sure he might cry. I reached up on my toes to kiss him. His hand locked on the back of my neck to hold me tightly as he returned the kiss.

When he pulled back, my cheeks heated as I looked up at him through my lashes. I was happy to see the stress melt away from his shoulders. Lee tries hard, I hated to see him weighed down when he was trying his best to do the right thing.

"Your girl held you down," Kim bubbled as she came over, pushing Lee and I toward the room I'd given to the baby. "I had my brother in here sweating,"

When we got to the room it was lit with the door opened. I stood in the door amazed myself. They had gotten so much done. I owed Kenny.

The crib was up, the dressers were in place, the rocking chair was together and in the corner. They had placed little stars on the ceiling and walls. I could see some of the clothes I'd bought folded in a laundry basket and more waiting to be folded. It looked like Kim had washed them all.

"You did all this for my baby?" Lee choked out.

"Yeah," I answered as I turned to look up at him. "I wanted him to have a place to stay. I didn't have baby things. I was worried."

"Yo, baby, you don't understand what this means to me. Lee has never had a room of his own," he said with a ton of emotion in his voice. "You did in a day what I couldn't get Rachael to do in month's. Lee's her son. Seriously Crystal, I love you for this. I know how much I hurt you, I didn't expect this."

"Don't I always take care of you?" I smiled up at him. "Baby, Lee's a part of you. I have to take care of him too."

Lee stood speechless. He cupped my cheek, gazing down at me. After a little while, he leaned to kiss my forehead, pulling me onto a hug. The baby started to rustle between us as Lee held him in his arms. It only took a few seconds for him to wake and start to whimper.

Kim rushed to Lee's side, pulling the baby from his arms. She rocked him, cooing at him to quiet him. Lee's hold on me tightened as soon as the baby was out of his arms. I let him rock me side to side while I peeked at his little one in Kim's arms.

His little face was so adorable as he cried. I figured he must have been hungry which reminded me that I needed to go shopping. I needed to get something for Lee to eat as well.

"I need to run to the store. I got everything but baby food."

"I got it. Kim you got little man for me?" he called after her as she headed out of the room.

"Yeah, I got him. You both can go," she replied.

"Thanks Kim," I chimed and looked up at Lee. "I need to get some things for you too."

"Come on, I'll take you." He said, a smile on those full gorgeous lips. "I love you, Crystal."

"I love you, too."

We rode to the grocery store so I could stock the house. I was a little low on everything. I wasn't expecting anyone at the house and my schedule was always so busy. The grocery store wasn't a priority. I had no idea what the baby needed, but Lee was great. I watched him place everything little Lee needed into the cart. I took mental notes so I would know for next time. I asked questions so I would know if the baby didn't like something or had allergies. Lee smiled more and more as I showed continued interest in his son. He eagerly answered all of my questions.

When it came to Lee I knew everything I needed to know. I filled up the cart with enough food and supplies to last at least two weeks. I thought about seeing if Manny would come back to work for Lee now that he was staying with me. I didn't mind cooking for Lee, but when Manny was around it was easier on my schedule and the both of us. We both have so much more on our plates now.

Once at the register, I reached into my bag to pay for the groceries. Lee pushed my bag away and swiped his card. I looked at him to wrinkle my nose at him. He leaned to kiss me on the cheek.

"And I'm going to need those receipts for the things you bought for little man," he said with a grin.

"Sure, I'll get that right to you," I teased.

I'd have to hide my receipt when I got home. Lee has been known for looking for my receipts to try to give me money back or pay my bills for me. I wouldn't have it this time.

"Yeah, I see that look. You didn't have to do that."

"Don't know what you're talking about. We went through this already, I take care of my man. Nothing else to talk about."

He chuckled as we loaded our bags into the cart. It was nice to see him look so happy. This was the most like himself I'd seen him since he showed up to the party.

When we got back to the house, Kim and Kenny had finished putting away all the baby things. The living room was back to normal, except for the baby swing I had purchased and a few toys Kim used to play with the baby. As soon as the baby saw me enter the house, he reached out his little arms for me. I looked at Lee and he beamed at me. Kenny took the bags I was carrying from my hands. I moved to take the baby from Kim.

Kenny and Lee went to get the rest of the things from the car. Kim followed me and the baby to the kitchen to unpack the bags and get dinner started for everyone. I unpacked with one arm as I balance the little guy in the other.

Baby Lee was so adorable. As I moved around unpacking things, he babbled as if having an entire conversation with me. He seemed a bit advanced for his age. If I was correct he should've been five months old. His ability to balance himself in my arms and the focused expression of his face as I talked to him was amazing.

He'd watch me say something, then try out his own his own little sentences. I chuckled listening to him intently as if I could understand his every word. He sucked in a breath and blew it out like a little man that had a long day at work.

"Okay, little man," I said. "We need to feed you and your daddy. I think I am going to call you LJ. You like that?"

He smiled and cooed at my words, bouncing in my embrace. His little chubby cheeks swelling with his smile. I laughed as his little gums came into view.

"You like it? Good, 'cause I like that too. LJ, I'm Crystal and this is your daddy's new home. I want you to know you're welcome anytime. And your new room will be yours no matter how old you get."

I started pulling out pots and pans to get dinner started. Lee came to wrap his arms around me from behind, playing peekaboo with LJ. The baby squealed with excitement, bouncing up and down with a jerky clap of his hands.

"Little man, you trying to steal my lady," Lee teased, as the baby got so excited he leaned in to place his mouth to my face, drooling down my cheek.

"Scared of a little competition," I jeered.

Lee laughed reaching to take the baby so I could use both of my hands. I missed LJ's presence instantly. He giggled in his father's arms trying to turn to find me.

I smiled before turning to focus on getting dinner ready. I had large T-bone steaks, cabbage, broccoli, and potatoes. I also wanted to make corn bread, knowing how much Lee likes the way I make it.

Once I had the onions and potatoes cut and thrown into the pans with the seasoned steaks, I placed them into the oven. Next, I worked on cutting the cabbage to steam it and tossed the broccoli in a pot. I saved the corn bread for last.

I worked as quickly as I could. I knew everyone had a full day tomorrow. Kim was a great help. She prepared the baby's food while Lee played with LJ on the couch. I could hear him giggling away.

"Thank you so much, Kim," I said as she stood in the kitchen with me. "I really appreciate this."

"Girl, please. Lee needs you more than you know. I'm just happy to see him happy."

"I'm so annoyed with her, Kim. How is she stressing him so much? I mean if she's after the money, doesn't she know if he gets hurt and can't play then the money is gone?"

I'd been thinking this over since last night. I didn't want to talk to Lee about it, but I needed to vent to someone. I mean, it made no sense to me.

"Crystal, that girl is stupid. She doesn't care a thing about either of them," Kim said in a low growl.

"I don't want to talk about it," I sighed.

I had changed my mind. Her not caring about Lee was one thing, but not caring about that sweet little baby was too much. That LJ was so cute. I wasn't ready to hear such selfishness.

"So you remember you have two heads tomorrow," Kim changed the subject. "I'm going to do Nichelle and Tammy's color and you got their cuts. We're training two new girls."

"I got you. I'll be in after going to the new place. I have one cut to do in Westchester in the morning, but I'll be in on time."

My words got me to thinking. Lee had practice in the morning. He'd need to get the baby to a sitter.

"Baby," I called into the living room. "Do you need me to drop LJ off somewhere in the morning?"

"Nah Ma, Kim is busy and my mom had plans already. She has some business to handle. I can't go to practice."

I frowned at his words. He's the quarterback. What was he talking about? From where I stood I could see the sadness on his face. My brows drew in as I worried how often this happened. This was getting more ridiculous by the minute.

"How often do you miss practice to babysit?" I asked trying to sound calm.

Kim snorted beside me. The sound sent ice through my veins. I knew Kim and Kenny never left Lee's life. They just never talked about him to me. They know everything that's been going on with him.

"This month four times so far. This will make five. So I'm about to be benched." He shrugged.

My heart crumbled. I could see the sag of his shoulders as his own words sank in. He looked broken all over again.

"Are you kidding me?" I said, throwing down the knife in my hand. "You're going to practice. I can handle the baby."

"Crystal, you're crazy busy. I can't ask you to do that."

"You're not asking. I'm telling you. Why are you missing practice? I mean, why haven't you gotten a nanny? This has to be costing you crazy money. I know you're being fined left and right."

I was fuming. All I could see was red. I wanted to put my hands on someone and that's not even me.

"I don't just want anybody with my son. I haven't had time to seriously interview all the people I was recommended."

I sighed, bracing myself against the sink. I tried to regain my composure. My thoughts raced as I formulated a plan. This made no sense. This time last year, Lee was a star player now he was one practice away from being benched.

"Okay, my brother's nanny is looking for work. His wife is a full time mom now and they don't need her. But they've been keeping her on until she finds something."

I know I was talking fast because I was thinking just as fast. I had to get this squared away. He couldn't throw everything he worked so hard for away for something that we could fix.

"She's great. She speaks several languages, my nieces and nephew love her. She's very picky when it comes to the families she works for. I can call and see if she will travel with me tomorrow that way I can keep an eye on her and see if LJ likes her. If she does well I can bring her here tomorrow after work and you can meet her.

"I know my brother has done reference and background checks on her, but I'll run my own. Meanwhile, I'll call around to see if anyone else has recommendations for someone really good."

I was already in the process of making mental notes and plans. I'm a fixer. It's what I do and I knew I could fix this.

"Are you sure about this?" Lee murmured.

"Yes. This is crazy, you're not missing practice. You can take my car. I'll use yours for the car seat."

I hadn't realized how hard I was slamming things until the baby started to cry. I felt bad that I had frightened him. I was just so damn frustrated. Rachael had single handedly undone everything Lee had worked for.

I made Kenny and Lee plates of food, making sure Lee's plate was piled high. When they were at the table eating, I went to get the baby tub to bath LJ. My sister-in-law swears by that lavender baby wash. I bought some in case LJ wasn't a good sleeper.

I called my sister-in-law while I got the baby's bath ready to ask about the nanny, Esther. I was in luck. My brother offered to give Esther a ride over first thing in the morning. He sounded annoyed about the Lee situation, but my brother loves me too much to argue with me.

Gregory Jr. does what makes me happy. I just hoped Lee was gone before he got here in the morning. Gregory is just as big as Lee if not bigger and he wasn't above threatening him.

Lee made himself a second plate as I got the baby washed and in fresh pajamas. LJ was such a happy baby. He splashed his little hands in the water while I washed him up. It was hard to be hurt when caring for him in the flesh.

I had LJ in my arms, rocking him when Lee entered the kitchen a third time. I thought he was going for other plate at first. Then I realized he was making a plate for me. He took my plate to the table before coming to get the baby and walked me over to have a seat.

He sat beside me, rubbing the baby's back. His eyes were trained on me while he watched me eat. Kim had finished off a plate and she and Kenny were getting ready to leave. I appreciated that she moved through the house to double-check that we were straight.

She checked to make sure she put batteries in all the baby monitors. Made sure the bottles were all out of the sterilizer. As she juggled her bag and keys she even changed the bag she packed for LJ's day tomorrow.

As Kim wrapped up, Lee and Kenny switched the cars in the driveway so Lee could take mine in the morning. I was so grateful Lee had such good friends and happy to now call them my own. I'd never be able to repay them.

I would have to thank Tamaria for the tip on the lavender baby wash. LJ was out like a light. I was placing him into his crib when Lee came back inside the house. Lee came in the baby's new room to find me.

I watched him kiss the baby goodnight. When he stood upright, he stopped to look around the room again. When his eyes met mine he had the biggest grin on his face. I reached for his hand to take him to our room. It was his turn to be pampered and put to sleep.

I'd planned to retrieve his luggage to unpack for him, but he had other plans. He pulled me into his arms and captured my lips with his. I started to giggle when he pulled my shirt over my head.

He continued to kiss me, unzipping my skirt. The fabric fell from my hips dropping to the floor around my feet. I could feel my body heating in anticipation.

Then he surprised me. He pulled off the rest of my things and led me to the bathroom. When we got inside, I noticed the bathtub was full of water and bubbles.

"Thank you for everything," Lee said softly. "This is the least I could do."

He lifted me up, placing me inside the water. He kept a tight grasp of my hand as I lowered down into the tub. Immediately, I felt the stress of the day melt away.

Although I was still annoyed with how out of control things had gotten in Lee's life, I let my mind relax to enjoy this gesture. Kim was right, Lee did need me. I was going to help him get his life back in order.

CHAPTER TWENTY

What We Want

Lee called me every chance he got the next day. He wanted to check on LJ and make sure he wasn't a bother to me. We were doing just fine.

LJ loved Esther. She was so great with children. She and LJ had been in the offices of the salons I had to visit most of the day.

Lee wanted to come get the baby, but I wanted him to go home and get some sleep. Esther and I had it under control. Kim had LJ in her arms whenever she wasn't working on a color job.

I could tell Lee was happy to hear LJ liked Esther. He asked to meet her so that he could interview her. I was happy it seemed we were on track to solving at least one of Lee's problems.

I'll admit, Esther had been a big help. I don't think I would have been able to make things work without her. I hate canceling on my clients but I would have if I had to.

When we walked into the house Esther was ready to change LJ and get into the routine of the evening. I was all for that, but I wanted her to meet with Lee as soon as possible. I showed her where the nursery was and we both worked on changing LJ and getting him out of the clothes he was in all day.

We made quick work of getting the baby washed down and changed. When we were done we headed back out to the living room. Lee walked out of the bedroom, looking as if he'd just woken up.

"Hey, Crystal," he yawned. "Little man, they treat you good today?"

He took the baby from Esther, playfully kissing his cheeks and nibbling at his little belly. LJ loved it, giggling up a storm.

"Hey baby," I chimed, moving to kiss Lee. "This is Esther."

"How do you do, Sir? LJ is a lovely child." Esther said with a wide grin on her face, as she appraised the interaction between father and son.

"Thank you. Would you like to sit so you can tell me about yourself?"

I loved the professional Lee. A man about his business is a sexy thing. He pulled one of my moves in changing his demeanor to handle his. I let my eyes roam over him taking in his commanding presence. When Lee has it together, he has it together.

"Sure," Esther answered.

We all made our way to sit in the living room. I sat next to Esther, realizing how intimidating Lee can seem. I didn't want to make her uncomfortable with us both glaring at her and grilling her. Lee sat in the chair across from us both with the baby on his lap.

"Esther would you please tell me a bit about yourself?" Lee said in a confident and professional voice.

"I have been in the business for ten years. I started when I was twenty-three. I have a Master's in Education, I speak several languages including Sign Language, Spanish, French, Italian, Mandarin, and Portuguese," she started. "I would be willing to teach LJ any of these but I will definitely be teaching him Sign Language and Spanish as I believe they provide a great foundation for learning and traveling. I cover basic learning skills and any programs you may want implemented.

"I'm very picky about the families I work for, but I believe I would like to work for yours. I prefer to be full time and live in, but I can do as I did today and care for LJ during the day as part time help. I believe Gregory gave Crystal my fees. I am among the most expensive, but I am also one of the best at what I do."

Lee sat back in his seat. I could see his thoughts turning. An intense look covered his features. I wanted to know what he was thinking, but I didn't want to pry. It was his decision. Esther is pricey, but I would help if necessary. Not hiring her would cost more.

When I talked to Lee earlier the money part didn't seem like a problem. He was more concerned with LJ liking her and how she treated him. I had her background check faxed to him. Tamaria was more than willing to provide a reference for her on top of the others Esther had furnished. She had been with my brother's family the longest. I could vouch for her. She had done wonderful with Gregory's kids.

"We can start with you working for a week as a trial. If things go well, we can talk about permanent employment. If you don't mind, it will be part-time like today," Lee started.

I totally agreed with his decision to hire of her a trial period until he was comfortable. I thought that was fair. However, I didn't understand why he only wanted her part-time. I bit my lips debating on whether or not I'd interfere. I seriously felt he needed to rethink that option so I couldn't hold my peace.

"Lee, not to interrupt you, but I thought you would want to use Esther on more of a full time basis. It would be easier with your schedule. On her and you," I pointed out.

"I would like to have her full time, but I wasn't sure that would be possible with my current living arrangements," Lee said.

I could see the concern in his eyes. I sighed, shaking my head at him. When I said I was here for him I meant it.

"Okay, I can take you to Gregory's to get your things and you can stay in the room next to the baby's. I will need to clear it out for you. It isn't furnished at the moment. There's an ottoman that unfolds into a bed for now, but if things work out we can furnish it as you like. Is that fair?"

I looked at Lee to let him know I was here to support him, not make things harder for him. Gratitude and relief filled his expression. It was the same look from last night.

"Yes, that sounds fair," Esther replied, turning to Lee she asked. "Is that okay with you, Mr. Johnson?"

"Yes. I would like if we can try this full time. I see your application listed your driving record and your license. Do you have a car?" Lee asked.

"I have my license, but I don't have a car at the moment. It wasn't really necessary with the Livingstons. They furnished transportation for me and the children."

"Okay, well I would like it if you would use the car Crystal used today for now. I would feel more comfortable if there is a car available to you," Lee responded.

My brows knitted with curiosity. My mind started to spin with his option for transportation. I figured he traded the Porsche in for the Mercedes he was offering her. I ran through my cars that were parked up to think of which would be practical for him.

Lee must have noticed my silent musing. He smiled and winked at me, causing me to tilt my head at him. I raised a brow at him in question.

"Would you mind taking little man with you to get Esther's things? I need to see if Kenny can take me to pick up my other car," Lee smiled in reply.

I laughed to myself. When we met, Lee was always so nervous about circulating money on cars. He called himself being conservative so that he wouldn't move out of his comfort zone. When we first got together I'd started to show him how to make things like cars and simple pleasures attainable, without touching his reserves.

"Sure, baby, no problem." I smiled.

My phone started to vibrate at that very moment. I picked it up to see it was a text from Jamie. I read the text and squealed quietly. Lee lifted a brow, returning the look I'd given him not long ago. This time I winked at him as I forwarded the text to his phone.

Taking a look at his phone as he pulled it from his pocket, a big grin stretched across his face. His eyes sparkled when they lifted back towards me. I could see my own excitement on his face. Our offer was accepted on the multi-unit property. We were in business.

Everything started to fall into place. It felt like a weight was lifted. All I needed to do now was get everyone on a schedule so this would work for us all.

CHAPTER TWENTY-ONE

To Be or Not to...

Two weeks had passed since Lee walked back into my life. I must say, the extra little baggage he brought along with him had grown on me something fierce. I was in love with LJ. I would be sad to see him go when his mother did decide to reappear.

I couldn't believe she hadn't even called Lee once. After the first four days, he stopped trying to reach her. He felt LJ was better off with him anyway.

I knew Lee was better off without her. He had been doing great in practice and is back to starting full-time. He even looked healthier now that I'd been cooking for him. I was able to get Manny to start back. He'd be starting in a few days. LJ even put on some weight with his cute little self.

It was another long day. Craig was almost finished with the new salon, so I needed to make sure things were in tiptop shape. I also had to show my face at both of the other shops. In all I had six heads to do. And if that wasn't enough I had a meeting with a new salon I planned to consult for.

Lee had been keeping himself busy outside of the house. He didn't like being in the house alone with Esther. The whole Rachael thing had him looking at everyone as a potential situation to avoid. He was so on top of all the pitfalls of being a star athlete after having a taste of where not thinking could lead him. He refused to get involved in anything else that could take him off track.

Lee pulled into the driveway the same time he did every night, just as I pulled in from work. He looked great getting out of the champagne colored Range Rover he drove. The huge bouquet of roses he pulled from the truck after getting out surprised me.

My eyes traveled over his body and face as he walked up to me. The man was just fine. His walk alone had me drooling as I took him in. I could tell he'd gone for a cut earlier in the day. Lee always looked good, but he was extra sexy with a fresh cut.

"Hey you," I purred.

"Hey," he smiled, dipping his head to kiss me.

Phew, did he kiss me thoroughly. My toes curled in my shoes. I was definitely going to need to change my underwear. My fingers were clinging to his crisp white t-shirt just to keep me from melting into a puddle on the asphalt beneath our feet.

"Yes, please," I breathed.

Lee lifted a questioning brow at me. "Yes, please, what?" he chuckled.

"More kisses just like that one. Please and thank you," I giggled.

"Not a problem," he crooned holding the roses out for me to inhale them.

I took a lung full of their fragrance, with a smile on my lips as I looked up at him through my lashes. A smile spread across his lips when I caught his eyes checking me out. He licked his lips while giving me a heated stare.

Placing a hand on the small of my back and holding onto the roses with his other hand he led me to the front door of the house. We walked inside together to find Esther on the couch singing and playing with LJ. She had all his attention until we walked into the door.

The minute LJ saw us he became all fussy, reaching out in our direction. I took the massive bouquet from Lee, freeing his hands up to get to LJ. LJ still wasn't satisfied. He looked around Lee for me, whimpering and stretching his arms out.

"Oh wow, little man. It's like that?" Lee laughed. "She has that effect on me too. I'm not mad."

Lee chuckled hard as he walked LJ over to me. LJ nearly jumped from Lee's arms to get to me. I placed the roses aside just in time for Lee to hand him to me, before moving behind me to envelope me in his arms.

"What did you do to my son?" Lee breathed in my ear. "Look at him. He's all happy now."

"I missed you too, LJ," I cooed as I laughed, kissing his chubby cheek. "Your daddy is just jealous."

"Nah. Let little man have his turn. It's mine later. Besides, he's gonna want to be my friend as soon as he sees you coming for him with those PJs."

My heart swelled to see Lee in such a great mood. His teasing continued as we stood cooing at LJ, making him laugh. Manny had already taken care of dinner so I had time to spare.

We took LJ to the living room to play with him for a little while before settling into our nightly routine. I was tired, but I couldn't resist that little face. LJ had me wrapped around his little finger just like his father. Those Johnson men made it so hard for me to say no.

Lee disappeared into the bedroom. I figured he went to take a nap. Esther was in the kitchen getting LJ's dinner ready as we played on the rug. She had been a great help so far.

Lee reappeared a little while later grinning and humming to himself. I started to wonder how his day went. He was in such a great mood. That sweet side of him came as he went into the kitchen to heat dinner up for us. I was so grateful. I was so tired my body hurt.

I swear I was ready to fall on my face. Just the small gesture of getting dinner on the table was so appreciated. I scratched my head, a sign of me getting sleepy.

When I looked into the kitchen, I could see Lee saying something to Esther that made her smile and nod. She came for LJ, taking him and his food out of the room.

I was starting to get suspicious now. Lee was up to something. I unzipped my boots, taking them off. Rolling my neck, I reached to rub the knots out, all while watching him.

"What are you up to Lee?" I quizzed.

"Who says I'm up to something? You look tired I'm just trying to help out," he beamed.

"Yeah, whatever." I giggled.

He face clearly said he was busted. He looked guilty as sin. I bust into more laughter the more I watched him.

"Come on, let's eat," he said as he took the plates over to the table.

Getting to my feet, I walked over to sit with him. He pulled my chair for me, kissing the side of my neck. His lips lingering on my skin, raising goosebumps on my skin. I turned my head to narrow my eyes at him. I took my seat but poked my lips out at him like my name was Arnold from "Different Strokes."

He was without a doubt up to something. I could see it in his eyes. I watched him with a cautious glare.

Lee sat across from me, before blessing the table. We both lifted our forks and started to dig in. I was so grateful to Manny. Not only was he saving me time, he was one of the best chefs I knew. Exhaustion hit and I began to chew with my eyes closed. I just needed a few minutes to relax and enjoy the food. When I opened my eyes, I found Lee's gaze locked on me. A seductive smile adorned those sexy, juicy lips.

"How was your day?" I asked.

"Nah, not tonight. I want to ask you the questions." His demeanor shifted. I could see determination lacing his russet colored orbs. "How was your day?"

"It was good. Long," I sighed.

"Did you miss me?" he asked, his eyes flicking over my face, before landing on my lips.

"Of course, baby."

"Good, I missed you too. I thought about you a lot today. Can I ask you something?"

"Sure," I replied, placing my elbow on the table and my head in my hand.

"Is this working? Am I making it better?" He zoned in on my face for my reaction.

"Yes. This is working. I am happy." I shrugged. "I can't say it doesn't still hurt a little every now and then, but having LJ here isn't as difficult as I thought it might be. I like having him here."

"Really? It doesn't bother you to have him here?" Lee asked still studying my face.

"Really. I love that little baby. How could I not want him here?"

He just nodded. "Okay." I watched him purse his lips, then return to his plate.

A few more minutes went by, before Lee looked up at me to stare again. I would love to know what was going on in his head. Too tired to eat another bite, I pulled my plate away to focus on him. I placed both elbows on the table so I could rest my head in my hands. My eyes remained on him, studying, wondering, trying to figure him out.

"I want to get full custody of my son. I went to see my lawyer today." He said slowly, again his eyes searched my face.

My smile consumed my face. I didn't want to get into that part of Lee's business, but I had been wondering when he was going to see that that's the best thing for LJ. Rachael could care less about that baby. He needs his father and Lee is a great dad. LJ loves him.

"That's great," I squealed.

"My lawyer thinks I have a good chance. Personally, I don't think she will fight too hard." He stopped to think for a minute as a frown set into his face. "I put the condo up for sale this morning. Rachael isn't going to live off me or my son anymore."

"I think everything will work out."

"What I'm about to say is not about LJ or Rachael. I wanted to say this for a long time. I just wanted to know that me having little man was cool with you."

"Okay, I'm listening."

He looked so perplexed. I wasn't sure what he was about to say. Whatever it was it made him look nervous and determined all at the same time.

"Crystal, I'm in love with you. I love the way you take care of me and the way you are with my son. In a matter of two weeks, you've helped get my life back in order. You always know how to make my dreams come true. With you I feel like anything is possible," he sighed, taking a long pause.

"I want to take care of you and love you the way you do me. I don't ever want to lose you again. The best way I know how to do that is to ask you. Crystal, will you marry me?"

I was so focused on his words, I hadn't noticed the ring box he had opened and set on the table next to me. My mouth dropped open the moment the words spilled out of his mouth. I just stared at him in shock.

I mean, I know we talked about this before. Before LJ, before I knew about Rachael, before all of this. It was where we were heading back then.

I didn't know what to say at first. I sat back in my chair, finally acknowledging the huge ring that screamed for my attention. My eyes flickered from it back to Lee's face.

He looked so nervous now. I wanted to answer, but I didn't know how. I clamped my hands on the back of my neck, taking a deep breath. I wanted this before, more than anything. At one time, I was ready to answer right away. Now, as the moment was before me, it was surreal.

Lee's face took on a look of pain. He looked down at the plate in front of him, as his eyebrows drew to the center of his handsome face. I tried to find my voice to speak.

When he looked back up at me, fire blazed in his eyes. He quickly snatched the ring from the table, getting down on one knee in front of me.

"Crystal, will you please marry me?" he asked again as his voice cracked with his words.

I had a sudden epiphany. I had to be crazy to let this man go. He loved me so much and LJ wasn't something he planned. We weren't together, he hadn't cheated on me. I think I had been more hurt that Rachael showed up at our home making the situation look worse than it truly was.

Lee provided for me when I need him to and he was willing to do whatever it took to do more. Lee is a great father to his son and he is a great boyfriend to me. I know he will be a great husband. I would be a fool to let Rachael and her scheming take this man from me.

"Yes," I finally blurted out.

Lee reached for my face, pulling me into a deep kiss. So much passion flowed from his lips to mine I thought I was going to faint. I wrapped my arms around his neck, laughter bubbling up on my lips.

What just happened?

My mind reeled as I tried to catch up. I think I was still in shock, but it began to set in slowly that I was engaged to Lee. I loved him so much. I couldn't believe he proposed.

"I love you. I promise to make you happy," he said against my lips.

He pulled away to place the ring on my finger. My heart started to pound in my chest as reality came with the weight of the ring on my finger. My eyes started to sting with unshed tears.

"I love you, too," I squealed as I looked at the ring on my finger. "Let's call my parents."

I jumped up from my seat, rushing to find my phone. I was so excited. I could barely find the number to dial it. I hadn't told my parents too much about what was happening between us in the past two weeks.

However, I know Gregory, Jr. and his wife had because my mom had been calling me non-stop. I'd just been dodging her calls.

"Hey Mommy," I squealed into the phone.

"Hey you. I've been trying to talk to you for weeks now," my mom grumbled into the phone.

"Is daddy around?"

"Yes, he's right here. He wants to talk to you too."

"That can wait," I sighed. "I'm getting married."

"What?"

"Lee asked me to marry him," I squealed.

My shoulders sagged slightly as I realized I wasn't getting the reaction I was looking for. I heard my mother on the other end of the line, rushing through telling my father what I'd said. I couldn't hear what exactly my father said back, but he didn't sound too happy.

"Coco, your father wants to talk to Lee. Is he with you?" my mother asked.

"Yes mommy but…"

"Coco put Lee on the phone," my father demanded.

"Baby, my father wants to talk to you," I said handing the phone to Lee.

Lee looked at me and sighed. He took the phone, pulling me into his arms. I reached up on my toes to kiss his lips.

"Hello, Mr. Livingston," Lee said into the phone.

It took only a few seconds for Lee's face to change and his arm to drop from around me. I looked up at him, searching for a clue as to what my father was saying. His features became more and more tense as he listened. After a few minutes, he walked out of the house still listening. He paced the driveway talking to my father for almost three hours.

When he came back into the house he handed me the phone without looking me in the face. I stood stunned as he went into the bedroom. I wanted to follow, but my mother was still on the line. She wanted to give me her own lecture. I had to plug the phone into the charger to listen to her.

We argued as much as I was willing to over the phone. It was a conversation I wanted to have in person with both of my parents. I needed to know what my father had said to Lee.

I was determined to find out. After another two hours, I was truly done talking. I needed to go see about my man.

When I entered the bedroom I found Lee lying in bed, shrouded in darkness. I changed for bed before I climbed in next to him. As I got closer, I could see the stress in his face. I was so upset with my parents.

"Baby, are you okay?" I whispered.

"Nah Crystal."

His voice came out strained. I could hear the hurt. It cut me to my soul. This was a good man that deserved happiness.

"What's the matter?"

"I don't understand. I'm trying to do the right thing. I made one mistake," he choked. My heart shattered when I saw the tears stream from his eyes. I had never seen him cry before. "Yeah, it was a big mistake that I will have to live with for the rest of my life, but I love my son. I take care of him and I make sure he's always okay. I stepped up to that.

"It's dudes out there that would've left LJ and Rachael on the street and said '*so what*'. I did what was right as a man. I tried to see if I could make things work out with Rachael and make little man a family, but she ain't the one for me. Rachael doesn't want nothing…nothing I want. Why should LJ have to live with that? All we did was argue.

"You are what I want, what I need, what I want for my son. You're more of a mother to him than Rachael ever has been. Am I wrong for wanting better for my son, for myself? I'm not trying to put my son off on you.

"That's my responsibility. I just want to be a man and make you happy. You don't deserve to have me in your heart, in your head, and in your bed, while I'm not willing to marry you. I thought I was doing the right thing. I really thought I could have you and make you happy.

"But it looks like I messed that up and everyone is going to make sure I know I did. It's like I'm going to have to pay for something that I'm trying to make right over and over again."

"Lee, baby, you didn't mess anything up. I'm going to marry you. You're not putting LJ off on me.

"How LJ got here has nothing to do with me. It was hard, but I understand that now. You made a mistake before us. I won't punish you or me for that. Neither should anyone else. It's none of their business.

"My father is only trying to keep me from being hurt the way he hurt my mother. He has a lot of damn nerve because I wasn't married to you when LJ came into the picture. Let him deal with his own skeletons, that's not your plate to eat from.

"As long as I want you and I want to be with you that is all that matters. I love you, Lee, and I love LJ. I'll be here for whatever you need and if that means helping you raise him, then I'm ready for whatever that means because I know you love me and you will take care of me."

I reached to wipe the tears from his face and kissed his cheek. He pulled me to his chest, hugging me tightly. I was truly exhausted by now. I wrapped my arms around him, holding on as firmly as I could. We fell asleep in each other's embrace.

CHAPTER TWENTY-TWO

Mirror, Mirror

When I woke the next morning, I was determined to set my parents straight. I called my assistant and cleared my whole day. I had LJ dressed before Esther was up and in his room.

They were coming with me for the day. Westchester was going to understand that this was my family. I wanted Lee and his son as well, if we got so lucky as to get custody of him.

I drove up to my parent's place and carried LJ right into the breakfast nook I knew I would find my parents in. They were both reading their papers and hadn't noticed me enter the room to take a seat before them. That's what happens when you have a house full of kids you learn to ignore.

"Good morning," I chimed after clearing my throat for their attention.

They lowered their papers, peeking at LJ and me. Both of their eyes traveled over my shoulder to see Esther. I painted on a huge smile as I stared back at them.

"I need to talk to the two of you," I said.

"We want to talk to you too," my father replied. "You've moved this man and his child into your home. You're taking care of them both…"

"Stop it right there," I cut him off. "This man and his child both have names, Lee and LJ. I take care of them both because they're my family. Lee takes care of me just the same."

"Coco, you don't need to be taking care of *Lee* or his son, *LJ*," my father started again pronouncing their names harshly.

"Okay, I'm going to stop you again. Daddy, I can't believe what you did last night. I don't know what all you said to Lee but I know you were wrong. Lee doesn't need you to beat him down. He looks up to you and right now he needs a mentor and support more than ever.

"He's trying very hard to do the right thing. He loves this little boy and does everything he can to make sure he's happy and healthy, even putting his career on hold. I don't understand why instead of helping him through this you want to make this worse for him and make him feel more lost than he already is.

"Daddy, you're no saint," I scoffed. "My other brothers and sisters are no secret. You of all people should be willing to cut Lee some slack. I'm marrying Lee and I will not let you break him down and make him pay for something he's more than paying for already."

I was just getting warmed up. I had a mouth full for my mother too. I truly couldn't believe them.

My father sat there with a frown on his face absorbing what I'd said to him. I was sure he knew I was right. My father had enough children to start his own freaking team, all younger than Gregory Jr. and in between the rest of us.

"Okay, Coco," my mother started this time. "But what about this baby's mother? Are you ready to deal with that?"

"If you were strong enough to deal with all of daddy's babies' mothers, then I can deal with one. You raised me to be as strong as you," I challenged.

"Yes, but I raised you that strong not to have to deal with this at all," my mother said, raising an eyebrow at me.

"Yes, but I can't help who I've fallen in love with and he can't help the mistake he made. Not now. That hasn't made me love him less." I was going to make them understand. "Mommy, you've allowed Daddy to bring his children here whenever they needed a place to stay and did what was necessary for them. This situation isn't nearly as challenging. Lee needs my support."

My father folded his arms across his chest and sat back in his chair. At this point I was sure he was done talking. I was going to get my way with him as usual. My mother looked at LJ, then me, releasing a deep sigh. She stared at LJ, letting a slow smile take over her face.

"May I hold my new grandson?" she beamed.

"I don't know. You two were mean to his daddy. He may not want to be your friend," I teased.

"Let's see," my mother said as she reached to take him off my lap. "You're quite handsome."

She cooed at him while bouncing him in her arms.

LJ reached to pull her glasses from her face, giggling at his new interest. My father even had a smile on his face as he watched the tiny monster steal my mother's heart.

That little face was full of magic. None of this was his fault. No one could hold a grudge in his direction after holding him in their arms.

We spent all morning and afternoon with my parents. My mom shifted gears, excited to have a wedding to plan. It was clear that I had made up my mind, there was going to be a wedding. LJ was down for his nap when Lee called.

"Hey, baby," I sang in the phone.

"Hey, Crystal. Are Esther and LJ with you? I called home and she isn't answering," he rushed into the phone.

"Relax. LJ is right here on my lap sleeping. We're all at my parent's."

"Oh," he grumbled.

"Why don't you drive up," I chimed.

"I don't think that's a good idea."

"Trust me, it's fine."

He paused for a minute. "You really want me to?" he sighed.

"Yes."

"Alright, I'm doing this for you."

"Thank you, and it will be okay."

"I'll see you in a minute."

It didn't take long for Lee to show up. When he did, you could see the tension all over him. I kissed him on the cheek as he wrapped his arm around my waist. He looked over to my mother's lap, where LJ sat drooling all over her hands.

My father stood up to cross the room, reaching out his hand for Lee's. Lee looked at me first. I winked at him in encouragement. He looked back at my father, taking his hand.

"Lee, I want to apologize. I was wrong last night. If Coco's happy, I'm happy. You're a fine young man. I shouldn't have tried to make it seem otherwise. Congratulations and welcome to the family," my father said as he shook Lee's hand.

"Thank you, Sir," Lee said a bit reluctantly.

"Congratulations, Lee," my mother chimed. "I can't wait until my little grandson here has brothers and sisters. I know they will be as gorgeous as he is."

Her words brought a big smile to Lee's face. He squeezed my waist and kissed the top of my head. I could feel some of the tension leave his body.

My parents brought out a bottle of champagne to celebrate our engagement and insisted we stay for dinner. Esther plans ahead just like I do. She had food for LJ and enough of everything else for our long day. When dinner was over we decided we needed to start the long trip home so LJ could get into his bed. We were getting ready to leave just when Lee's phone rang.

"Hello," Lee murmured in to the phone.

A deep frown took over his lips. *So Rachael is finally surfacing,* I thought to myself. I wondered when that was going to happen.

"I'm not," Lee replied to whatever she said.

"Rachael, my son's belly is full. If there's no food there you're a grown woman find some," he hissed at his phone.

"No, I'm not bringing you any money. Look, we need to talk. You need to meet me tomorrow, twelve o'clock at that restaurant downtown."

He paused for a quick second to listen. He face read of pure disgust. The grip he had on his phone looked like he was going to snap it in two.

"You'll find out when you get there. Just make sure you show up," he said before pausing again.

"Fine, take a cab and I'll pay for it when you get there," he sighed at her response.

"In case you were wondering, Lee is fine," he hissed into the phone.

He hung up on whatever her retort was, shoving the phone in his pocket. His expression was so angry, I didn't bother to say a word. I just handed him the baby and followed him out to the cars. Lee placed LJ in his car seat, before coming to give me a long hug.

I could feel him hurting. Despite my parents apologizing and making him feel welcome tonight, their words had already done their damage. Rachael's call hadn't helped at all. Lee needed a minute to breathe.

CHAPTER TWENTY-THREE

True Colors

I slept in the next morning. I was too worried about Lee and his meeting with Rachael. I had hoped she wouldn't demand to have LJ back. That would truly break my heart. I have grown so attached to him. I was glad it was my day off.

When I finally rolled out of bed I showered, then went straight to LJ's room. Esther had him on a play rug, singing the alphabet song while playing with toy cars. She's so good with him. I sat on the rug with them to push the cars around for him.

I spent a good hour in the room with them before Lee came in. His expression was ten times worse than last night. I stood up from the rug we were planted on, moving over to him. He locked his arms around me, holding on for dear life.

After a few moments, he pulled me from the room to head for ours. When we reached the room he paced the floor as I sat on the bed watching him. He began taking off his suit, still too angry to talk yet. I gave him time to calm himself so he could speak.

"You know she didn't bother to ask about him?" he started. "She was willing to walk away from him for three hundred grand."

"What?" I gasped in disgust. "You offered her money?"

"No!" He stopped to rub his temples. "My lawyer explained to her what I wanted. Before he could finish, she said she would leave and I could have him for three hundred grand. I'm not giving her shit!"

"Are you serious?"

"Man, Crystal. She tried every way she could to get money out of me. My lawyer had her sign to give permission to tape the conversation and she still was bold enough to try to negotiate money."

He stopped pacing to come lay down on the bed. My heart hurt for him. I couldn't believe my ears.

"Baby, it's going to be fine. At this point, I'd pay her to go away," I giggled, trying to lighten the mood.

"The whole time I was there, I just wanted to come home to you. I love you."

"I love you, too. Tell me how to make it better."

He looked over to me, motioning for me to come to him. I crawled closer to him, leaning in to peck his lips. He reached for my leg, pulling me to straddle across his stomach. Reaching up he pulled my face down to his. The kiss started out soft as he caressed my back.

"I want you to have my baby," he said softly.

"Okay, well we better hurry up and plan the wedding. Then, I'll give you all the babies you want," I laughed.

"You know that's not what I mean," he said as he began to undress me. "I want to give you my baby."

"Lee, we can wait. We have LJ," I insisted.

"No, that's not the same," he moaned. "I want to have a baby with you. I don't want to wait."

"I don't know," I breathed as he kissed my neck, making it hard to stay focused. "We should talk about this."

"Come on, Crystal. Let me try. If it doesn't happen then cool, but I want to try. I want a baby with you. That's all I keep thinking about. I want you to give me a little girl."

"Lee, are you sure you want to do this?" I moaned. "I think we should wait."

"Nah, I want this now."

His lips covered mine, taking my words away. I whimpered into his mouth. His tongue came out to flick against my chin. My back hit the mattress with a bounce as he flipped us.

Looking down at me with hunger in his eyes, he started to release the buttons on his dress shirt. I licked my lips, reaching behind my back to release my bra. I tossed the garment aside, watching as his chiseled chest came into view.

Lee tossed his shirt behind him before dipping to take one of my hardened peaks into his mouth. I cupped the back of his head, bowing off of the bed. His mouth was warm and wet against my skin. The swirl of his tongue had me grinding and writhing beneath him.

I bit my lip and groaned. His fingers hooked into my panties snatching them from my hips. I gasped in shock. My nipple popped free from his lips as he looked up at me with determination and a heat I'd never seen before.

I could tell he met business. My mind raced as he reached to unbuckle his belt. I'd never slept with anyone without protection. This was a new level in our relationship.

"Do you want to see my last physical results again?" he offered, sensing the shift in me.

"No, I saw them already," I said softly.

He placed a hand on my belly, running his fingers up the center of my body. I shivered at the feel of his rough hands on my smooth skin, the contrast a total turn on to me.

"I thought about being inside of you the whole way home," he crooned.

"Baby," I pleaded.

"Shh, I've got you," he replied.

His fingers found their way between my legs. Lee kept his eyes on me as he strummed my body to a fever pitch. I rocked my hips, wanting and needing more.

He sucked that full bottom lip into his mouth. Watching Lee play with my body had to be one of the sexiest things in the world. I could feel my climax building.

When he reached down to stroke himself to the rhythm of his hand taunting my pussy, I completely fell apart. His big hand wrapped around his thick, long length was a sight worth coming for all on its own. So I did.

His lips were back on mine. I wrapped my legs around him as he coaxed me to. My mouth parted in a silent scream as he slammed into me.

He rolled his big body into me as if dancing to a sexy slow song. I dug my fingers in his back to anchor myself. It felt so good I was in tears. Tears of pleasure and disbelief that sex this good was even possible.

"Lee," I cried.

"You feel so good, baby. Give me that pussy. Show me who it belongs to," he breathed.

"It's yours," I promised.

"Show me," he commanded.

Swiftly, I used my strength to push him onto his back, rolling with him. I steadied myself with my hands on his stomach. Planting my feet onto the mattress, I went to work.

My head fell back, my hips circled as I lifted up and dropped back down. I took advantage of all the length I had to work with. I could feel him deep inside me.

I bit my lip to keep from screaming out. It wasn't too fast or too slow. We'd set a pace that worked perfectly. Lee's hands cupped my breasts, guiding me to move up and down on him.

"Damn, girl," he growled. His hips rolling up into me.

"Yes," I purred leaning forward, I dropped down, clinched my walls around him, and twerked my ass on him.

"Fuck," he hissed between his teeth. "I'm tear that ass up."

At least he gave fair warning. He plucked me from his lap, placing me on all fours. My face dropped into the bedspread as I hollered into it. His grasp on my hips, the drilling of his strong strokes from behind. It was all so overwhelming.

"Yeah, that's it. Come all over me," Lee purred, slapping my ass three times.

Right, left, right, his strikes sent my ass bouncing. He roared out his own release as his hot seed filled me. My eyes bulged in my head.

It was a strange feeling, but it triggered multiples to run through me. I anchored my back, which Lee took as an invitation. He rode through both of our climaxes still semi hard.

His arms wrapped around me as his pace turned to one of coaxing. As if he were stirring and calling for something more than an orgasm from my body. He soon came to full mass and rocked my body until squirting into me once more.

"We're not done," he chuckled.

"I figured," I said lazily.

CHAPTER TWENTY-FOUR

Our Little Girl

Of course, Lee got what Lee wanted when it came to Crystal. He wanted to try for a baby and I gave him his wish. It had been two months and I still hadn't gotten pregnant.

However, wedding plans had been in full swing. We were planning a May wedding. Lee didn't want to wait until the following year and May was perfect for him with his off-season schedule.

My parents are letting us use their place for the ceremony and reception. Our mothers were becoming best friends as they helped me plan the wedding. Lee's mom, Sharon is the sweetest woman ever. Her happiness came from seeing her son happy. She's shared with me on many occasions how much she loved the way I cared for Lee and LJ.

We are getting married the week after LJ's first birthday. I had become so attached to my little monster. It was clear to see how much Lee loved that.

Lee insisted we start teaching LJ to call me mommy. At first, I wasn't sure how to take that, but as the second month hit with no call from Rachael, I was all for it. LJ needed someone to act like his mommy. Since I seemed to be the only one willing, I don't see why he shouldn't call me mommy.

LJ seemed to love me as much as I loved him. I found myself rushing home from work just to see him. I loved the way his little face lit up when I walk through the door.

I usually got to bond with him the most on the weekends that Lee had away games. We tagged along with Lee a few times to the states that had nice places to take LJ. Like the museums, aquariums, and stuff like that.

Lee was totally back on track with his game. Physically he was back to himself as well, nice and healthy. Chances of winning the super bowl were looking good for the year. Lee's stats are amazing. He was totally focused. His endorsements are stable and more offers were coming in.

We were becoming a real happy little family. Esther helped us to keep our family running smoothly. She turned out to be the perfect choice for us. LJ was learning so much from her.

Life was great on almost every front. I was on track with the salons and the new projects were well under way. We were a well-oiled machine.

"Crystal," Lee called from the bathroom.

"Huh?" I replied as I tickled LJ's tummy, giggling with him.

"You think you can take LJ to see my mom tomorrow? She's been asking me to bring him up this week, but by the time I pick him up from home and get there it would be too late," Lee called into the room.

"Sure, babe. I have the day off. Are you going to come up after practice?"

"Yeah," he answered as he kissed me on the cheek and sat on the bed next to LJ and me. "You sure you didn't have something else you needed to do?"

"Nope, I was planning to spend the day with LJ anyway."

"Thanks, Crystal."

"I guess it's your bedtime, Little Man," I cooed at LJ.

LJ made a face at me as if he understood what I was saying to him. He wasn't done playing with me yet. I lifted him into my arms. His little hands grabbed my cheeks, pulling my face to him. He mashed his little face into mine.

Laughing, I got up to take LJ to his room. I found Esther sitting on the couch waiting for me to bring him out. LJ was a little fussy when being handed over to Esther, but he calmed down when she started to sing to him while rubbing his back.

LJ raised his little hand up to wave at me as I blew him a kiss goodnight. I just adored the little smile that stretched across his face. He was such a sweet boy.

I reentered our bedroom to find Lee with a sexy smile on his face. His eyes remained on me as I climbed back onto the bed with him. I beamed at him, crawling up his body before settling across his lap. I shifted forward to lie on top of his chest. His arms incased me in his strong hold, his lips moving to kiss the top of my head.

"What are you smiling at?" I chuckled.

"You. You're great with him, you know that? My little girl is going to be lucky. She needs to hurry up so LJ doesn't keep taking up the spotlight."

"Your little girl knows her mommy doesn't want to walk down the aisle looking like a blimp. She'll come when she's ready."

"Nope, my little girl and I know her mommy will look beautiful pregnant or not. So she's going to be good and show up for her daddy," he replied, reaching to lift my face to his so he could kiss me.

"So does that mean her daddy wants to try again?" I chimed as I wiggled in his lap.

"You already know," he breathed, running his hands down my back to cup my globes in a firm grasp.

Lee didn't have to ask twice. He would get his chance to try again. I rocked against him as his strong palms kneaded my ass, moving to spread my cheeks only to release his hold and slap my ass. I moaned, shifting to get him free of his pajama pants.

My mouth watered for him. My eyes twinkled as I thought of all the ways I planned to torture his sexy body until he came. Knowing he would fight the entire time to keep from groaning and grunting too loudly.

I licked my lips as his massive length came into view. I was already wet and ready. It didn't take long to get him in my mouth and bring him so much pleasure his toes curled.

I don't know what I enjoyed more—watching him come undone from my mouth or lying beneath him as he took my body to places that should be outlawed. Our lovemaking silenced my thoughts and doubts. Being in the arms of the man I loved so much outplayed everything else.

I had to admit I was a little nervous about trying for a baby, but I was sure I wanted one with Lee. With the wedding around the corner, I tried convincing myself that if it happened it wouldn't be such a big deal.

After all, my career was definitely intact and Lee's was on the right path as well. It was only after he brought me to the brink of sanity and the edge of bliss that my thoughts started to consume me again. His hot seed filling me was a fiery dose of reality.

I couldn't help lying there in his arms trying to rationalize things as he combed his fingers through my hair. I'd told myself for the last two months that I wanted a baby as much as he did. It wasn't just me giving him what he wanted.

Sometimes, I thought it hadn't happened yet because I was so twisted up about whether or not I wanted a baby so soon. Or was it because I'd fallen into a pattern of doing what I know would make Lee happy. Then, I thought about LJ and how much I love him.

A million times over I'd wished that he was my own. Whenever that thought occurred I had no more questions. I want to be the one that gives Lee his first little girl. Either way we were both getting what we wanted.

"Baby?" Lee mumbled, "We're going to need a bigger house."

"Are you ready for that?" I replied as he broke into my thoughts.

"I want to at least start looking. We're already outgrowing this place. With another baby, it's going to be tight in here. We don't need to live like that. I want to give you a bigger place," he answered as he traced circles on my back.

"You know we don't have to rush if you don't want to, this place is fine for now. LJ likes it."

"I don't feel like we're rushing. This place is cool, but it's not someplace I've given you. You know what I mean?" he sighed, taking a brief pause. "I feel like I need to make a home for you and LJ. I'm focused now and everything is lining up the way it should. I sold the condo so I want to look for a place we can call ours."

"This is ours," I replied, lifting my head to look up at him. "Lee… LJ and I are at home."

"Nah baby, you're not getting it. I need to know I'm making you safe and secure. This house is yours. I love you for welcoming me and LJ here and making us feel at home, but I *need* to give you more."

"Okay, if that's what you want," I answered, placing a kiss on his chest. "We can start looking."

"I thought we could look in Westchester or New Jersey this time," Lee suggested.

"Alright, that would put me sort of in the middle of everything either way."

"If you want to stay close to your family we can do Westchester."

"Lee, did you not notice I'm nowhere near them now?" I laughed. "It has nothing to do with my budget."

"Okay," he chuckled.

My fingers caressed his chest as I snuggled closer to make myself even more comfortable against his body. Lee tightened his arms around me, changing the subject to the wedding. We talked a little while longer before we both drifted off to sleep.

CHAPTER TWENTY-FIVE

Time to Relax

I woke up to help Lee out of the door the next morning. Afterwards I jumped into the shower and dressed myself, before heading to LJ's room to get him ready. I wanted to get an early start on the day to make it to Connecticut in time to spend a good portion of the day with Lee's mom. Esther was always up early so I didn't have to worry about her.

Ms. Sharon was up and waiting for us when we arrived. LJ of course was excited the minute he saw his grandma. She spoils him the same way she spoils Lee. He was in grandma's arms receiving hugs and kisses the minute we stepped into her house.

We sat in her living room while playing cartoons for LJ. Ms. Sharon could throw down so I was happy to see some biscuits on the coffee table for us to munch. Lee's mom makes sure to feed you anytime you come to her house. Lee always joked that she stopped cooking when he hit the NFL, but I'd never seen her leave him without something to eat if she was around.

"I'm happy you came, Crystal," Ms. Sharon said. "I've been wanting to talk to you alone."

"Really? What did I do?"

"You can relax," she laughed. "You know we never talked about what happen between you and Lee. I wanted to let you know how much you mean to my son."

"Oh... you know you really don't have to do that."

"No, I think I do. Lee was so lost without you."

"Trust me. I wasn't doing any better than he was."

"I'm sure of that. I see the way you two are together. It broke my heart that I couldn't help my son out of that situation. I had to watch him lose himself and I wasn't sure he was going to make it back. But now he's so happy. I see him becoming a better man from it all."

"Lee's a wonderful man. I think that's what I've always loved about him. He's so determined and ready to learn and grow. I just want to help him get to where he wants to go. That's the least I can do for him. He makes me so happy."

"I just want you to remember all of that when things gets tough. Raising another woman's son—especially one as trifling as Rachael, isn't going to be a cakewalk. You need to remember why you love Lee when things get tough."

I loved Lee's mom and the wisdom she always brings. I had a feeling I would need her advice someday. I let her words sink in.

"Thanks. I'll keep that in mind," I said as I smiled at her.

We smoothly changed the subject to the wedding and the schedule for LJ while we're away on our honeymoon. My mother offered to split the time with Ms. Sharon while we're away for the two weeks. Esther would be there to help them both out.

Not that either of them would give her a chance. They're in love with him just as much as I am. Kim even offered to take a few days if they need her to.

We hadn't realized how much time had passed until Lee walked in with flowers in his arms for both of us. We were both in the kitchen, working on dinner and some cookies for LJ. I have to say, Lee made my day when he walked in. Lee is so good looking everything stops when he enters the room. Not to mention, his cologne set my mouth to watering.

"Hey you," he whispered into my ear as he wrapped his arms around me. "Thank you."

"No problem. I had a great time with your mom."

"Alright, that's cool. Listen, we haven't had time to ourselves in a minute. My mom is going to watch LJ. I'm taking you out."

"Your mom cooked."

I turned to face him.

"Crystal, she did all that to send something home with us. She knew my plans."

My heart melted as his boyish smile took over his face. I should've known he was up to something. He always gets that hand in the cookie jar expression on his face right before he surprises me like this. I suddenly remembered seeing it that morning.

"I love you," I giggled and wrapped my arms around him.

"I love you too. Now let's get out of here before Little Man sees me."

I ran to get my things while Esther held LJ's attention. Lee and I were in his truck on our way out for a real date, something that hadn't been as easy as it used to be. I didn't mind but Lee is always apologizing for not being able to just get up and go.

Esther is great but we hated taking advantage of having her. We worked so much as it was and she has LJ during those long hours. We hated the thought of throwing social hours on her. Not to mention, I liked being around for LJ whenever we're not working. Going out on a date was a nice change though.

"So where are we going?" I asked excitement settling in as Lee drove out of the gates of his mother's community.

"I made some reservations at a restaurant and I have tickets to that concert you were talking about," he smiled and peeked over at me.

"Seriously, Lee, that concert has been sold out since the ticket box opened. How did you get those?"

I was totally ready to burst. I'd wanted so badly to go to that concert. All of my R&B faves were going to be there. I'd thought about going a few times. Kim had even offered to babysit or come with if Lee wasn't interested.

"I've had them for a month. I knew you wanted to go."

"Thank you," I squealed leaning to kiss him on the cheek.

"No problem, baby. That's not it though."

That sexy smile grew. I shifted in my seat to lean against his arm as much as I could. The smell of his cologne luring me in.

"What else?"

I felt like a little kid eager about a trip to Disney or something. When Lee wants to spoil, he knows how to spoil. My mind had a million ideas of what he might've planned.

"My mom is going to keep LJ overnight. I booked us a suite for the night. I had Jennie rearrange your schedule for tomorrow. I thought we could have a little night to ourselves and do a little shopping tomorrow."

"Um, shopping? Would that be shopping for a house?" I laughed.

"Maybe," he chuckled.

My eyes softened as I looked at him. He truly looked happy and content for the first time in a long time. You would never know we had just gotten back together only two months ago. It was like Rachael never happened.

I took in the moment, second chances didn't always come so easy. Everything had started to move so fast. It was like the plans we once had were just on hold and now we had pressed play. LJ was just a surprise bonus to the plans. A surprise that no one seemed to mind now that we had him.

My love for Lee and LJ was an overcast to the mess with Rachael. The fact that she had disappeared made it easier by the minute to forget it ever happened, and nights like this made it all the more forgettable.

Dinner was wonderful. The man I fell in love with shined through every action and gesture Lee made. I loved that he was willing to answer anything that I asked and in turn allowed me to make him the center of my attention.

We left out the talks of business and the busy things in our life. It was a time to bring the pace down to a romantic night between the two of us.

The concert was incredible. Lee had gotten us exclusive seats, with an amazing view. After a while, Lee caught on that I was sneaking out to the lobby to check on LJ. He teased me about loving his son more than I loved him, but I could tell he was happy I'd checked on our baby.

Lee was no better than me. As soon as the concert was over he jumped on the phone with his mom to make sure everything was okay before we made our way to the hotel. I'm sure the few times I saw his phone light up it was because he was sneak texting her as well.

I was stunned when we got to the hotel. Lee pulled two pieces of luggage from the trunk. He had taken care of everything, including packing me a bag. The suite was beautiful. From the moment we walked in, my breath was taken away.

Lee had champagne and strawberries set up on a table for us. There were more flowers like the ones he brought to his mother's house for me. It was all so romantic and sweet.

"This is so beautiful," I chimed as I threw my arms around him. "I'm so happy I'm marrying you."

"That makes two of us. I want you to go relax. I just need to make a call."

"Um, you wouldn't be checking on Little Man again, would you?" I teased.

"No," he laughed. "I packed you something special for tonight. You'll see it in your bag."

"In that case, when you're done you can meet me in my favorite place to relax."

I stood on my toes to kiss him before heading into the bathroom to run the tub. Once the bathtub was filled, I undressed and slipped in to wait for Lee. I hadn't realized how much I needed this night.

With all the running I've been doing, I never stopped to think about how tired I've been. The warm water on my body told me exactly how much I needed a time out. Aches I hadn't noticed started to release and soothe beneath the water.

I was completely relaxed by the time Lee entered the bathroom wearing absolutely nothing and carrying two glasses of champagne. I couldn't help the smile that consumed my face. All I could think of was how all that chocolate belonged to me.

In just a few months, I would be married to him for the rest of my life.

I took the glasses while he slid into the tub with me. It only took seconds for me to be wrapped in his arms where everything was always perfect. It felt nice to just sip champagne and relax with the man I loved. This is what kept me with Lee. He always knows how to make me happy and he had been getting better and better at it.

"You okay, baby?" Lee said softly in my ear.

"Yes, perfect," I sighed. "I needed this."

"I know. You've been all over the place."

"I just want to get things right and then I'll slow down."

"Yeah right," he snorted. "You don't know how to slow down. I would like it if you did though, just a little. Maybe it's time we get you another assistant."

Just like Lee, always thinking about how much I'm doing, like he does any less. He just took on coaching Kenny and Kim's little cousin's Pee Wee league team. Between that and a few charities he agreed to sponsor he was booked solid. He needed an assistant as much as I needed a second one.

"Yeah, but then I'd have to train them. I don't know…it seems easier to just do what I know on my own."

"True, but you can't do everything forever, especially not the way you've been trying to handle my schedule and yours. The new salons are almost ready and things are taking off for you. I just want you to think about getting some more help."

"Okay, I'll think about it. Maybe after the wedding."

Lee laughed and kissed my neck. "Nah, you need to get some help before then."

"Don't worry about it. Kim and Kenny have been taking care of things at that salon and I'm handling everything else.

Once this grand opening is over next month, I'll be set for a minute."

"I can see that getting you to slow down would be like getting me not to play with a broken hand," Lee sighed.

"Oh no, you wouldn't be playing," I snorted. "Just trust me, baby. I have it under control, us, the baby, and work. Don't worry, I don't miss a beat."

"Alright, I'll make a deal with you."

"Okay, what's the deal," I sighed and nestled into his chest.

"Once you're pregnant, we're getting you two new assistants. For now, I'll hire someone to take care of my schedule and all the extras I have."

"Um, let me think about that," I turned to look up at him. He groaned and rolled his eyes. "No, seriously. I'd need to train them on how to make sure your business is being handled right."

Lee laughed hard, squeezing his arms around me. Burying his face into my neck he inhaled deeply. Goosebumps covered my skin, causing me to bite my lip and smile.

"I love you, but I can make sure my business is being taken care of. Let me worry about that."

I gave in after a little while longer. I knew Lee was right, but I liked handling things my way. I figured it was time to compromise though, if I wanted to have everything in my life working smoothly. Lee was only trying to do what was best for me. Just like I always did what's best for him. It felt nice to have someone looking out for me and my best interests.

When the water cooled, Lee started to get out of the tub. I grinned to myself. I moved quickly, lifting to my knees and turning to face him. Speaking of taking care of my man. I needed to thank him for the night.

I placed my hands on his thick thighs to stop him from exiting the tub. He looked down at me with lust in his eyes when I leaned forward and licked a trail up his inner leg.

I stopped short of my prize, turning to repeat the action on the other side. Lee cupped my chin lifting my face. I looked up at him through my lashes.

"You don't have to," he said tightly. "I did this for you."

"Boy, please. I'm about to suck this dick for me," I chuckled.

His head fell back as laughter rumbled in his chest. All of his laughter died when I covered his length with my mouth. He groaned looking down at me with the sexiest look on his face. He licked those sexy lips as his eyes narrowed on me.

I worked my head back and forth, soaking him in my saliva. I turned my head side to side, making sure my lips and tongue touch every inch of him. I wrapped one hand around him as I steadied myself with the other on his waist. I pumped and sucked, pulling loud groans from his lips.

He popped free from my lip and I tilted my head to go for a taste of his balls. His fingers locked in my hair. I took a long lick from is root to his tip.

"Aw, hell nah," he groaned.

It the next move I was sailing through the air until we were face to face. My legs were wrapped around his waist and my core was impaled by the delicious treat I had just been having a taste of. I purred in appreciation at the way he stretched me.

"This might be a long night," he breathed in my ear.

"Bring it, baby."

"Always."

The next morning we slept in for a change. Lee had booked us an appointment with a developer in New Jersey for late in the afternoon. When we did get up, we dressed and headed out to their office.

Nervous energy buzzed through us. We'd never bought a house together before because we could never agree on a place we both liked. There was always something one of us wanted that the places didn't have. Going to see a developer to possibly start a new build would be a way for everyone to get what they wanted and needed.

We drove to a few potential locations to see what our land options were. We found the perfect place for our new home after about four tries. I couldn't believe how things were falling into place. Lee didn't waste time putting in a bid for the land. We were in the builder's office picking blue prints before I knew it.

Everything finally made sense. I understood why Lee wanted me to have more help. We were now going to have a brand new build on our hands along with everything else. That didn't scare me though. I was ready.

I wanted everything that Lee had to offer me. LJ, the huge new mansion, and our new three acres of land. It was my dream come true. Nothing could get in the way of what we were building it was all perfect by divine design and intervention if you asked me.

Again

Lee had been trying to get me pregnant for months now. He gets this frown on his face every month when he realizes it hasn't happened. He knew my cycle better than I did.

I didn't mind that it hadn't happened yet. I didn't want to be pregnant walking down the aisle anyway. At least, that's what I'd been telling myself. I gave Lee the same excuse but a part of me gets disappointed too.

The wedding is in four weeks and we were stronger in our relationship than ever. The house was coming along great. If they continued at the rate they were moving we'd be in the house in time for the holidays, which would be perfect for LJ. LJ had gotten so big and he was very smart.

Lee hadn't heard a word from Rachael in months. So it was a surprise to us when she called asking to see LJ. I thought maybe the mother in her was finally waking up with his birthday coming up.

Lee didn't care what her reason was. He didn't want to be bothered with her. He decided to meet her in the park with Esther and me along with him. I wanted no parts of it.

I had no intentions of going. The only reason I changed my mind was the look on his face when it was time to leave to meet her. I wasn't going to let him drive LJ around looking like that.

The whole ride over he cursed and grumbling under his breath. I tried to distract him by lightening his mood, but it wasn't working. I'm a little relieved we are finally at the park. However, now Lee's shouting for me to get out of the car with him.

"Crystal, you're coming with me," he growled.

"No, Lee, I'm not."

"Crystal, get out of the car," he hissed as he opened his door to get out.

I watched him storm around to my side. Esther had already climbed out with LJ. Lee ripped the door open, the look on his face told me I better go with him to keep him from killing Rachael. I stepped out of the car and he slammed the door shut behind me.

Lee took LJ from Esther, heading toward the location where he agreed to meet Rachael. When we got closer to the benches, I noticed her seated on one. She turned to see us coming toward her at the same time. Racheal stood up and I thought my head was going to explode.

This selfish heifer went and got herself pregnant again!

She didn't want to take care of the one she had and she went and trapped some fool into getting her pregnant again. I wanted to kick her ass. I've been wanting to for a while, but I really wanted to whip her tail now.

Lee looked down at me, his face tightening even more. He kissed LJ's forehead as he narrowed his eyes at her. When we got to her, she looked me over, then looked at Lee. Her face had the nerve to be pinched like she smelled shit.

"Lee, you got so big. Let me see you," she called to LJ.

He didn't even look her way. He clung to Lee with his head on his father's shoulder. I wanted to tell her his name was LJ, that's why he wasn't answering her.

"Lee, honey," she said in this phony voice, as she rubbed his back. "Come to mommy."

LJ lifted his head and looked at me. He turned a little to look in her direction, then looked back at me again. I knew he was trying to figure out what she was talking about. I was the only mommy he had known for months.

"Honey, you're not going to come to mommy?" she tried again.

This time LJ leaned to reach for me. I reached to pull him from Lee's arms before he tried to jump from them. He placed his head on my shoulder, staring at a pissed Rachael. I rubbed his back, unintentionally drawing Rachael's attention.

"Oh, wow. So are you going to try to take this one from me too?" she snorted as she rubbed her belly.

"Excuse me?" I said.

"You heard me. You stole my son, are you after this baby too."

"Okay, you know what I haven't stolen anything from you. And what do I want with that baby?" I barked.

"Esther, please take LJ to the swings for me," Lee called through his teeth.

Esther came to take LJ with her. Lee wrapped his arms around my waist. It felt like he was trying to restrain himself by holding onto me. I placed my hand on his chest, looking up at him.

"Rachael, what do you want? You haven't called or wanted to see LJ in months. Now you're calling?" Lee seethed.

"I wanted to let you know you have a little girl on the way," she beamed.

I felt like I was just kicked in the stomach. My hand clutched the front of Lee's shirt. This wasn't happening to me again.

Lee promised me. He promised me I would have his little girl and he promised he would never hurt me like this again.

"What the fuck are you talking about?" Lee snapped. "Rachael, I'm not playing with you."

"Lee, I'm seven months. It's a little girl. I was thinking we could name her Lily or maybe Leeha," she said smugly.

I needed to sit. I moved numbly to sit on the bench. Once I sat I looked down to see my hands were shaking. I stared at the ring on my finger that was screaming at me.

'Stupid. You fool!'

It was all I could hear. I looked up at Lee, but the tears had started to blind me. I blinked to see his face was enraged and in pain at the same time.

"That's not my baby! Rachael, don't call me no more. If you want to see LJ, you call my lawyer," Lee bellowed.

He reached down to pull me from the bench. He barked for Esther to follow us to the car. When we got to his truck, I climbed into the back to sit with LJ.

I didn't say a word the entire ride home. Lee was so angry, I don't think he realized I wasn't sitting next to him. Esther had taken my place. I sat and watched LJ.

I'd made my peace once, I didn't think I had it in me to go through this again. The fact that Rachael could be telling the truth seared my soul. She and Lee lived with each other for months. The girl slept in his home, in his bed. That could very well be Lee's baby. Knowing that crumbled my heart to pieces.

I had decided. I had helped to make my house LJ's home. I wasn't going to make him leave. I would go. Lee and LJ could stay as long as they needed to. It was the only home LJ knew. I wouldn't rip him from that.

I was saying my good byes. I would miss him. I tried to hide the tears from him. LJ's very perceptive for a child, especially one his age.

When we pulled up to the house, I kissed LJ on the forehead and jumped out of the car. I quickly made my way into the house. I entered the storage room to get my luggage. I took my bags to my bedroom, placing them on the bed. I opened them wide so I could throw things into them as fast as I could.

The tears were running hot and fast. I heard Lee enter the room and close the door before he walked up behind me. He wrapped his arms tightly around me. I broke down at his touch.

"What are you doing?" he said into my hair.

I couldn't answer. I sobbed, trying to pry his arms off of me. I could've easily hurt Lee, but I don't want to. I just wanted his hands free of me.

"What are you doing?" he asked again. "That's not my baby, Crystal." I started to cry more as his words served as a reminder.

He reached for my suitcases, pushing them to the floor. Turing me around in his arms, he lifted my face. Kissing me softly, he looked in my eyes.

"That's not my baby," he repeated.

Gently laying me down on the bed, he covered me with his body. He kissed my neck, reaching for my legs to trail his hands up my thighs. I couldn't help the moan that escaped my lips as my body betrayed me. No matter how much I was hurting, Lee's touch always set me on fire.

"That's not my baby," he moaned in my ear.

Lee slowly undressed me, before undressed himself. I wanted to believe him, I wanted this to be okay. I wanted him to make me feel better.

"You hear me, Crystal? That's not my baby," he panted. "I love you. I wouldn't do that again."

I panted and writhed beneath his expert touch. A part of me wanted to trust his words, I needed to. I wrapped my legs and arms around him tighter and relaxed under him.

"I love you. You're the only one I will ever make another baby with," he groaned. "I love you, Crystal. You hear me, baby? You, only you."

Tears rolled back into my ears. I dug my fingers in his back, gasping for air. It felt like my senses were heightened as every inch of him moved in and through me.

His kisses rained all over my face and neck. I clung to him needing to feel safe in his arms. I always felt safe when he made love to me. I would believe anything he said when he made me feel like this.

My mind tried to reel against my body. The betrayal of it all. I wanted to deny him but his touch demanded that I receive the pleasure that was Lee.

"I love you. I will always love you," he groaned into my ear.

His fingers found mine, lacing with them. He brought our interlocked hands above my head, pressing them into the mattress. I stopped fighting and allowed his love to course through me.

It was all so intense. I lost my sense of direction. Up was down and down was up, Lee was the center of everything whether wrong or right. I was anchored to him for the time being. My body opened for him in a new way and he made love to a vulnerable part of me.

"Lee," I started to moan his name.

Only Lee could make me feel this way. I was so in love with him. I think that was my problem. I could never see straight because I loved him so much.

"I love you. You have to feel how much I love you. I love you so much. I'd never destroy us. I'd die before I hurt you ever again," he promised. "Believe me. I love you."

I sobbed as I broke down beneath him. He wrapped me in his big arms and continued to come at my body and heart like a wrecking ball. He was relentless and I was helpless. I couldn't think straight, all I knew was Lee.

After two hours of Lee causing me to forget what I had planned to do, I curled up in a ball on the bed. He layed next to me, but when he reached to rub my back, I pulled away. He sat up on the bed, staring down at me for a few minutes. Jumping up in frustration, he went into the bathroom.

The moment the bathroom door closed, I let out a loud sob. It was blood curdling. I heard Lee punch something in the bathroom followed by something breaking. I continued to let out loud sobs. I heard the shower come on in the bathroom, but didn't move. Instead, I cried some more.

I realized this was my chance. Lee hated to see or hear me in pain. He couldn't handle it, he would stay under the water trying to drain out my cries as long as he could.

I got up, throwing on the first thing I could put my hands on. I tossed a few things in a bag. Next, I ran for my car.

I needed to get away from Lee to think straight. I couldn't stay with him and trust myself. I didn't know if I was hearing the truth or if I just wanted to hear the truth.

I needed time and space for clarity. I needed a moment to breathe without him. I'd get through this, I just needed time alone.

CHAPTER TWENTY-SEVEN

The Truth

I went to stay with my parents. I told them that I needed to stay with them because I had caught some bug. I didn't want to make LJ sick. That worked for the first two weeks because I did nothing but cry in my room. When I did come out, my face was all puffy and I looked a mess as if I were sick.

I cried about Lee, missing LJ, and the fact that I wasn't sure if Lee had another baby that wasn't mine coming into this world.

Lee would call all day, every day. He sent flowers once a day without fail. I wouldn't answer his calls and I trashed the flowers when no one was looking. My mother thought Lee was such a sweetheart for sending flowers while I wasn't feeling well. As far as she knew he felt bad I had to leave our home because of LJ's well-being.

By the third week, my mother started to look at me a little funny. I told her the wedding was two weeks away and I thought it would be a good idea if I stayed close to her to help. That worked for about two days.

Once she noticed I'd begun to down a pint of ice cream a day and I wasn't working as much as I usually did, she started to give me side eye and began to pry. Her hawk like attention had zoned in on me. I did my best to cover the situation up.

It didn't help that the flowers started to get in my head so much they made me nauseous. I couldn't help but throw them out right away to keep from losing the contents of my stomach. I seriously couldn't stand the smell in my room.

My mother caught me throwing the flowers out one morning and started with a round of a million and one questions. I tried to dodge them as much as I could, but she asked one too many and I blew up.

It was so out of character for me. I locked myself in my room and cried some more. I needed to get out of the house.

My assistant informed me that Lee showed up at the Westchester salon every day. I knew he knew where I was, and just like me, was refusing to involve my parents. I figured I could go to the newest salon, but I thought that would be the next place he would look to find me.

The last place he would expect to find me would be with Kim and Kenny. I needed to cut some hair and fast. It was the only way to soothe me.

I threw on a pair of grey leggings, a black tunic top with a grey leather belt, and a pair of stiletto boots. No need to look like crap just because I felt like it. Trying to be slick, I took out my grey Jaguar. It was a car Lee knew little about, one of my father's gifts.

I hoped it would keep him from finding me at the shop if he passed. He'd be looking for a car he knew. All I knew was I needed to get my moody, 007, ass to a station and lose myself.

I called Kim and told her I'd be in. She promised to line me up as many heads as she could. I made it to the shop in record time. Kim had two girls waiting for me to start with. I jumped right into my work. These girls were lucky. I actually work better under stress.

Kim was pretty busy when I got in, thankfully. She didn't have time to grill me. Although, I could see in her face she wanted to.

Once the word got out that I was in the shop, girls were lined up to get their hair done. I was plenty busy. I only stopped to inhale something to eat in between styles.

I noticed when Kim slowed down for the day. I knew she would be heading my way as soon as she could. I told the receptionist I wasn't taking anyone else after the girl in my chair. I wanted to finish the last two cuts and get away from Kim.

I found myself missing LJ as I mindlessly cut hair. I'd usually be in a rush to finish up to run home to see him. I missed his little face when it would light up as I walked through the door.

Esther had taught him Sign Language, which led to him already talking a bit. He would be squealing mommy whenever I came home. The thought almost brought tears to my eyes.

As if thinking about it wasn't bad enough, once I started my last cut, lo and behold, Lee walked in the salon with LJ in his arms. I felt sick to my stomach. I looked at myself in the mirror and I swear I looked green. I was so glad this girl was only a touch up. I would have her out of my chair in twenty minutes or less.

Lee stood talking to Kenny as he watched me. I could feel his eyes burning a hole through me. I couldn't stop fidgeting or peeking up into the mirror to catch a glimpse of him, each time confirming his eyes were on me.

LJ was fast asleep in his arms. It took everything in me not to rush over and take him into my own embrace. I wanted to go hug, kiss, and smell him. My little baby had a scent unique to him—something I hadn't noticed until I couldn't hold him every day. I missed him so much.

As I finished the cut, LJ started to stir in Lee's lap as they sat in the barber chair next to Kenny. I walked the girl to the register to get her change.

When LJ fully woke, he looked around at his surroundings. His face lit up as if he knew he would find me in the room. He scanned the shop and when his eyes finally met mine he squealed.

"Mommy, Mommy!" he beamed.

I returned his bright smile, rushing over to pull him from Lee's lap. I hugged him so tight. This was the worst part of all of this. My heart would heal some day from walking away from Lee, I'd hoped. But I didn't think it would ever heal from walking away from LJ. I felt no better than Rachael.

"Hey, LJ, I missed you, sweet pea," I sang.

He giggled and put his little fingers on my face, pulling me in to kiss his cheek. He is such a sweet little boy. I had to fight back the tears.

"Muah," I said as I kissed his cheek. "You love mommy, LJ?"

"Mm, hmm," he chimed and nodded his head.

"We both love and miss mommy," Lee whispered in my ear as he wrapped his arms around me.

"Please don't," I said, trying not to let LJ see my irritation.

"Crystal, we need to talk. LJ misses you, I miss you. When are you going to come home?" Lee asked.

"LJ, mommy, needs to talk to daddy go ask Auntie Kim for a cookie," I told LJ kissing his cheek and placing him on his feet.

I watched as he ran over to Kim, pulling on her apron while calling out cookie. Kim looked at me and laughed. LJ was in her arms in the next minute. Kim disappeared with him into our office.

I smiled after them. We were all still floored by how smart he was. He seemed to have gotten bigger while I was away.

"Lee, I'm not going to do this with you," I hissed at him.

"Do what? That's not my baby. Stop letting Rachael rip our home apart. LJ really misses you. He sings about you all day," Lee said and reached for me.

"Lee, I said I'm not going to do this."

"Why can't you believe me? I manned up to my son. I'm not taking the wrap for a baby that is not mine."

"Lee...I," I couldn't get my words out. I felt my stomach turn.

Lee reached for my waist, but I pushed his arms away to run for the bathroom. This was too much for me. I needed to get away.

I made it to the bathroom just in time. I emptied my stomach, feeling the stress weighing down on me. I felt horrible. Kim tapped on the door, calling my name but I couldn't even answer.

I tried hard to relax and think of something else to pull myself together. It took a little while, but I was calm enough to move to the sink to wash my face and hands. Splashing cold water on my face helped a lot.

I stepped out of the bathroom to see Kim standing by her station. Lee had taken a seat in my chair, a scowl fixed on his face. I went to collect my things so I could go home. As I approached my station, Lee reached out for me, but I brushed his hands away trying to get to my things.

"I just want to make sure you're okay," he said sincerely.

"I'm fine. All of this is stressing me out is all," I grumbled.

"I don't understand why you're letting this stress you when I did nothing wrong."

"Whatever Lee."

"Are you okay?" Kim said from behind me.

"Yes, I'm fine."

"You haven't been looking so good today. Do you need to go see a doctor?"

"Kim, I just have a lot I'm dealing with. I'm fine."

"Okay, I don't like getting in you guys business, but I think it's time I did," Kim said.

I laughed to myself. She was probably the one that called Lee. Kim is always in his business, which has placed her always in the middle of mine.

"Kim, there's nothing to talk about," I grumbled.

"Yes there is. You have been avoiding Lee for almost a month and you guys are getting married in less than two weeks," Kim demanded.

"There's not going to be a wedding. I'm going to tell my family tonight."

Lee tensed in the chair, grabbing the armrests as if they were keeping him in the chair. His expression looked like he wanted to kill someone. Kim grabbed my arm to turn me so I would look at her.

"Are you serious? Over that liar? You're kidding?" Kim yelled.

"How do you know she's lying?" I shouted back at her.

"Trust me, I know. Lee isn't the one lying, that baby isn't his," Kim demanded.

I started to feel queasy again. A burp bubbled up in my throat. My mouth filled with water.

"I don't need this, it's too much. Please just let me leave," I cried.

"You need to listen before you ruin—" Kim started to say but I pushed her out of the way. I knew I wouldn't make it to the bathroom. I quickly kneeled to the floor in front of the closest trashcan. I didn't think I had anything left.

My face was covered in tears and sweat. I felt Lee's hand on my back, rubbing as I held my head in the can. This was so embarrassing.

"Mommy," LJ called as he came to mimic Lee's gesture.

"You alright, Crystal?" Lee asked voice filled with concern.

"I told you this is too much," I gasped, wiping my face with the wet towel Kim handed me.

"Seriously, I don't think that's the problem," Lee whispered in my ear as he continued to rub my back. "I can tell by what you're wearing you're late."

I looked at him like he was crazy. I tried to process his words. I began to do the math in my mind. My head started to spin so fast, I was having a hard time thinking or breathing.

He was right. If it was that time I wouldn't be dressed in leggings it was a hard fast rule for me. But was he right about the timing?

Lee was like a watchdog for that time of the month. I was absolutely horrified when I realized the truth of his words.

I snatched away from him to stand up. I stood up so fast, I felt dizzy. Lee quickly stood to catch me as I stumbled back. I frowned and pushed his hands from me. I didn't want him touching me. I couldn't believe this was happening now.

"Crystal," Lee called as I backed away with a look of disgust on my face.

I quickly turned and ran for the office. Kim was right on my heels following me. I needed to get as far away from Lee as possible. I felt like such a fool for the millionth time. How did I let him talk me into this? I had no idea what I was going to do.

Kim followed me into the office and closed the door behind her. I walked over to my desk and braced myself against it. I couldn't even fight the tears because it only made me nauseous.

Kim moved closer to hand me some mouthwash from her desk. I rinsed my mouth, wishing I could make the bitter taste of reality go away as well. Kim wrapped her arms around me as I cried.

"Why now Kim? How did I let him get me pregnant? What was I thinking?" I whimpered.

"Oh, Crystal, you're pregnant?" she squealed. "That's great."

"This isn't great. How am I supposed to move on if I'm having his baby?"

"Move on? Girl, you need to stop trippin'."

"I want to believe him, but I don't know if that's me just wanting to believe him or me knowing I should," I cried. "They lived together. He slept with her. He told me once that he tried to make things work for LJ."

"Lee didn't get Rachael pregnant again. That's not his baby," Kim demanded.

"What makes you so sure about that?" I almost yelled at her.

"Because I know what you don't know. Yes, Lee tried to do right by LJ. He tried to give Rachael a chance. That no good heifer violated him and his house," Kim said through her teeth.

"What are you talking about?" I demanded.

"She had Sean up in his condo and he walked in on them," Kim explained. "Lee and Sean got in a big fight. Lee was pissed. He knew that Sean had pushed him to get with Rachael and bad mouthed you the whole time so he could get at you. To top it off, Sean was up in his place with Rachael after everything that happened with you. Lee whipped Sean's ass," Kim laughed.

"Are you serious?"

"Girl, Lee got locked up over it. He didn't want you to know. The team kept it quiet. But that wasn't it. Lee stopped messing with her and started telling her to find a place to stay.

"That's when she started the disappearing acts. Telling him she had emergencies. The first time, she disappeared Lee called me all upset because he needed to get to practice. He didn't have anyone to watch LJ. I told him I was on my way.

"I'd been at KG's. He had let the guys have a groupie party the night before. We'd stayed locked upstairs most the night.

"When I left, I had to step over passed out bodies on my way out the door. Right before I got out of the house I saw Rachael's naked behind passed out next to this guy KG just signed to the label. Bitch told Lee she had an emergency the night before. Some *emergency*.

"I told Lee as soon as I got to his place. Lee wouldn't put a pinky next to her, let alone get her pregnant again. Lee can't stand that girl. She's seven months pregnant, Crystal...trust me that's not Lee's baby."

"Kim really?" I sniffled.

"Yes mommy. You need to go out there and get your man. Let him take care of you and that little baby in your tummy," she chimed. "He loves you girl. Lee would never hurt you like that."

I pulled Kim in for a hard embrace. I trusted her. I knew she would tell me the truth. She was the first person I called when Rachael showed up the first time. She understood how I felt about Lee and how much I loved him.

I thought about what Lee's mother told me. I had to remember that I loved Lee when things got out of control. I took time to get myself together before going back outside.

Kim wrapped her arm around my waist, placing her head on my shoulder as we moved to leave the office. As she opened the door, Lee came into view. He stood in the threshold holding LJ in his arms.

"Mommy," LJ sang, "You tay?"

I kissed him on the cheek and laughed. His little face was filled with concern. His brows pinched looking just like his father.

"Yes, LJ, mommy is okay. She is just going to give you a little brother or sister," I said as I looked at Lee.

Lee searched my face cautiously. I wrapped my arms around him and LJ as I lifted up to kiss him. His hand landed on the small of my back, lifting me into his kiss.

"I'm sorry," I whispered.

He shook his head at me, placing his forehead to mine. We remained silent for a few moments. I felt so ashamed for not trusting him. We still had a lot to learn, but I knew we could make it.

"I love you," Lee moved to say into my ear as he rubbed my back. "Let's go home."

CHAPTER TWENTY-EIGHT

Crystal

I pushed all thoughts of Rachael and her lies out of my head and started to live my life again. Lee was telling the truth and she just couldn't stand the fact that Lee wanted to marry me while she couldn't get a fifty-cent frank out of him.

We make a very successful power couple together. That's what we both were looking for. I had to evaluate the best parts of Lee. There were more of those than there was drama.

I did like his mother warned me. I remembered why I loved him. When I found out I was pregnant I knew it was meant to be. Lee and I deserved to be happy. We deserved to have everything we dreamed of. Less than two weeks after that day in the shop, I became Mrs. Lee Johnson.

~*B*~

Lee

Making me the happiest man in the world. She wasn't just pregnant with my first daughter but she also gave me my second son. She always gives me more than I expect. As you can see, we're expecting again.

See, I felt if I told you my story you would understand what awaits you out there. I love my wife and almost lost her and everything else because I lost focus for a single moment. The game will play you just as hard as you play it.

You young athletes have to stay focused if you want to survive and have a real life, not just the fantasy of the game and the life it provides. Crystal was what I needed to keep from losing myself to the game. Some of you will not be that lucky to know when you have it as good.

I just want to warn you not to make the mistakes I did. Having a real woman by my side helped me focus on the game and got me that championship in my third season. However, I have known what the wrong woman is like and how costly that can be.

Most of all, you should remember that not all advice is good advice. Not everyone giving it has your best interest in mind. I made the mistake of taking advice from someone that had none of the things I wanted, but wanted all of the things I had.

I hope Crystal and I said something that will help you stay focused and out of trouble. If not, I hope one of the other stories you hear will show you the truth about the life you're entering. It's great to enjoy the experience. Just make sure the experience isn't taking the joy from you.

Are there any questions?

ACKNOWLEDGMENTS

Star is an old love of mine. Some of you may have read the original. I laughed my way through rewrites. Good lord, have I grown. I still love Lee and Crystal though and I'm happy with the polish I was able to add to them. Hoping to add more to their collection in the future.

To my family. Yes, I'm talking to all of you as readers. Thank you for being you. Your love and support means the world to me. Your encouragement and emails mean the world. They are always right on time. Thank you for watching me grow and encouraging me to do so. I don't take you for granted.

This book is for my mother. When she passed, I made her a promise. It took me a while to get back on my feet and see my way forward, but I'm making that promise come true. Mommy do you see me? Love you forever.

Many people talk that talk but won't walk that walk when called to. Faith takes commitment to the journey. It requires pushing even when you no longer want to. But when you root yourself in faith it's a beautiful thing. You remember what's for you is for you. No one can take that away and God will make sure it is so. Thank you, Lord for wisdom and faith. May your will be so.

On to the Next!! *Man, there are a million books in the works, stay tuned. LOL*

ABOUT THE AUTHOR

Blue Saffire, award-winning, bestselling author of over thirty novels and novellas, writes with the intention to touch the heart and the mind.

Blue hooks, weaves, and loops multiple series, keeping you engaged in her worlds. Blue and her husband live in a house filled with laughter and creativity, in Long Island, NY. Yet, the city still calls to her to come on back for a visit.

Wait, there is more to come! You can stay updated with my latest releases, learn more about me the author, and be a part of contests by subscribing to my newsletter at www.BlueSaffire.com

If you enjoyed Star I'd love to hear your thoughts and please feel free to leave a review. And when you do, please let me know by emailing me at TheBlueSaffire@gmail.com or leave a comment on Facebook https://www.facebook.com/BlueSaffireDiaries or Twitter @TheBlueSaffire

Other books by Blue Saffire
Placed in Best Read Order

Also available....

Legally Bound

Legally Bound 2: Against the Law

Legally Bound 3: His Law

Perfect for Me

Hush 1: Family Secrets

Coming Soon...

Other books from the Evei Lattimore Collection Books by Blue Saffire